ONE GIRL

WINNER OF THE 1998 WILLA CATHER FICTION PRIZE

The Willa Cather Fiction Prize was established in 1991 by Helicon Nine Editions, and is awarded annually to a previously unpublished manuscript chosen by a distinguished writer through an open nationwide competition.

The judge for 1998 was William Gass.

ONE GIRL
A Novel in Stories

SHEILA KOHLER

HELICON NINE EDITIONS
KANSAS CITY AND LOS ANGELES

Grateful acknowledgment is made to the editors of the following magazines
and anthologies in which these stories first appeared:

"Luck," *Massachusetts Review*; "Peaches and Plums," *Ploughshares*
"Cracks," *Paris Review, KGB Anthology*; "The Original," *The American Voice*
"Ambush," *Yale Review*; "The Bride's Secret," *Redbook*
"Structure," *Yale Review*; "Light," *The Quarterly*; "Trust," *The Quarterly*
"Africans," *Story Magazine, Best American Short Stories of 1999*
"Water Baby," *New Letters*; "On the Money," *Columbia Magazine*
"Correspondence I," *The Quarterly*
"Correspondence II," *The Quarterly, The Antioch Review*

Cover painting: Balcomb Greene, *Sunrise*, 1978 (detail)
Book design: Tim Barnhart
Author's photo: Bill Hayward

Helicon Nine Editions is grateful to the National Endowment for the Arts,
a federal agency, and to the Missouri Arts Council and
the Kansas Arts Commission, state agencies, for their continued support.

LIBRARY OF CONGRESS CATALOGING-IN-PUBLICATION DATA

Kohler, Sheila
      One girl : A novel in stories / Sheila Kohler. -- 1st ed.
      p.   cm.
      "Winner of the 1998 Willa Cather Fiction Prize."
      ISBN 1-884235-29-8 : (acid-free paper)
      I. Title
PR9369.3.K6405   1999
823--dc21   99-37346
                                                                              CIP

Manufactured in the United States of America
FIRST EDITION
HELICON NINE EDITIONS
KANSAS CITY AND LOS ANGELES

This book is for my beloved husband Bill

I

Like the sweet apple which reddens upon the topmost bough,
Atop on the topmost twig,—which the pluckers forgot, somehow,—
Forgot it not, nay; but got it not, for none could get it till now.

II

Like the wild hyacinth flower which on the hills is found,
Which the passing feet of the shepherds forever tear and wound,
Until the purple blossom is trodden in the ground.

—Sappho
(trans. Dante Gabriel Rossetti)

CONTENTS

PART ONE *Childhood*

13 Luck

20 Peaches and Plums

PART TWO *Adolescence*

29 Cracks

41 The Original

PART THREE *Courtship and Marriage*

49 Ambush

63 The Bride's Secret

79 Structure

84 Light

88 Trust

101 Africans

110 Water Baby

121 On the Money

PART FOUR *Death*

137 Correspondence I

150 Correspondence II

157 ABOUT THE AUTHOR

PART ONE

CHILDHOOD

LUCK

THE MAN SITTING NEXT TO HER in the cinema is watching her, not the film. She is wearing her best green silk dress with the sash her mother has tied too tightly around her thin waist. She has slapped her cheeks to bring some blood into them, as her mother has told her to do.

The man is eating chocolates. She hears him crinkle the wrapping papers and throw them onto the floor. She glances at the big box on his knees. The man lifts the lid, and she sees one of the square ones in its ruffled paper.

The man whispers, "Excuse me, I hope you don't think I am rude, but is a young lady like yourself all on her own in the cinema?"

She pushes her hair back from her face and goes on watching the film. She has seen it. She has seen most of the films in the cinemas in the town.

There are many people here. The cinema smells of popcorn and unwashed socks and the faint tang of urine. It is hot, and the cigarette smoke is caught in the light of the projectors.

The man turns to her again. He whispers, "And where is Mother?"

His mouth opens again a little, and he says very softly, "Well, I say, and she lets a young lady like yourself go out to the cinema, all alone?"

Sidonia shakes her head, and her blond hair sways around her shoulders. It is not plaited as it usually is. She has washed it that evening, and it shines.

"And Father?"

"Dead," she says. The man sighs and shakes his head with sympathy. She can see in the flickering light of the cinema that he has dark hair slicked back from his forehead with brilliantine.

He offers her a chocolate. She looks down at the square one.

Just as Ava Gardner starts singing, "Fish gotta swim," the man whispers, "Very pretty blond hair."

Sidonia pops the square one into her mouth, as Ava sings "Can't help lovin' that man of mine."

That summer began as usual, with the thin Indian waiter running down the polished red steps in his starched uniform and inclining his turbaned head elegantly to welcome Sidonia's mother to the hotel. The hotel seemed to float between the blue African hills and the hot sky like a vast white ship.

The waiter piloted them through the revolving door and the pools of shadows in the lobby, past the potted palms, the portraits of ladies in long dresses and feathered hats, and the fountain in the shape of a small frog, the water trickling from its maw. He threw open the door with a flourish as he said, "A suite this year for Miss Sidonia, as she is quite the young lady now, isn't she?"

Sidonia smiled at him and looked up at her mother's face, but her mother only glanced distractedly at the fruit basket with

its orange bow wrapped in cellophane on the table by the window and the view of the sea behind it. Her mother said the trip
had been very hot and fanned her cheeks with her lace hand-
kerchief. She asked him if there were any guests of interest this
year. He said he was sure they would be arriving soon. Then she
kicked off her high-heeled sling-back shoes, collapsed into a
chair, and asked for a double whiskey and soda with lots of ice.

The days went by like a string of smooth beads. Called by
her mother in the early morning, Sidonia stumbled half asleep
across the darkened room and curled up beside her. Her mother
extracted her plump bosom from her silk nightgown and offered
Sidonia the dark nipple, stroking Sidonia's long blond hair until
it was time to order breakfast. Mornings, Sidonia jumped over
the big breakers on the noisy beach, pretending to bump into
the fat ladies so that she could pinch their behinds, while her
mother lounged under the shade of an umbrella. They lunched
in the vast dining room. No one else was there except the
Indian waiters and an elderly woman who slipped pieces of fruit
surreptitiously into her knitting bag.

Sidonia liked the way the tall Indian waiter bent his turbaned head toward her mother and manipulated the short sharp
knife with his long blunt-tipped fingers, making radishes bloom
into roses, or folded white napkins so that they soared magically
into twin peaks with valleys full of flowers, all the while talking
to Sidonia's mother about who was to be the winner at the
Natal races. Sidonia's mother sipped imported beer, the froth
lingering on the dark hair of her upper lip. Her mother told him
that she had always been lucky in life. The waiter smiled and
said if she followed his tips, she was sure to continue to be.

Sidonia noticed how her mother removed her shoes under
the table and rubbed one slim, stockinged foot against the
other as she talked to him. Her mother told Sidonia that in
India such men did not have to be waiters, but were maharajah

with vast fortunes and costly jewels. Her mother always slipped him money to bet on the races, the winnings to be divided between them.

In the afternoons while her mother slept, Sidonia descended into the vast green park with its flat flame-trees and brightly colored flowers. She swam up and down the long freshwater pool alone. Sometimes she slipped her arms out of the straps of her swimming costume and folded down the top and felt the cool water against her flat chest. She went on swimming until her fingers began to crinkle like crepe paper. Then she lay flat on her stomach in the shade of the acacias and the straw-roofed bathing huts and listened to stories about love on her radio.

In the evening, they dressed for dinner. Her mother made Sidonia dress up in a different dress every evening. Her mother would say, "Slap your cheeks to bring some blood into them. It will make you look less sallow," staring at Sidonia in the mirror with a critical air.

The vast dining room was very quiet and hot. Only the Indian waiters moved about among the few guests, serving endless courses in their white uniforms, like ghosts. The only sounds were the roar of the sea and the chink of china.

Her mother sipped her wine and sighed and mentioned Sidonia's dead father. Her mother would say, "That was the happiest time of my life." She told Sidonia how generous her father had been, how he had covered her with jewels, showing Sidonia the big blue-white one she always wore.

Often her mother told Sidonia how very beautiful she, herself, had been as a girl. She had had so many beaux she had been obliged to give some of them to her sisters. Sidonia would gaze at her mother's soft dark curls, her dark melancholy eyes.

Sidonia would search the dining room for fair-haired men with blue eyes like her father's.

• • •

When the lights come on, Sidonia rises to go. The man stands up, and asks if she would mind if he introduced himself. He hopes she will allow him to befriend her, he says, extending his hand. He has long fingers, slightly stained at the tips. He is wearing a blue blazer with gleaming gold buttons.

He says he would be happy to give her a lift. "Won't you give me the honor of taking you home, young lady? Surely it is not safe for a young lady like yourself to be out in the street alone after dark." Sidonia thinks the man speaks a bit the way people do in books. She notices his white teeth.

The man asks Sidonia where she is staying. He says, "Ah, I know the hotel well. I stayed there as a child, when we came out from England." He adds that he would love to stop by some time and see Sidonia, but why not strike while the iron is hot?

They are out in the street now. The people from the cinema disperse, and the lights on the marquee go out. The narrow street is quiet, Sidonia's hands are damp, and her dress sticks to her back.

The man says he does not want to interfere, but there are few taxis about, and he has a perfectly good car just waiting to take her home, pointing at a sporty red convertible across the street.

Sidonia admires the car. She stands in the shadows, looking down at her best green shoes with the bar across the instep and the buttons that are so hard to do up.

The man says he knows what she is thinking. He would tell a pretty daughter like her exactly the same thing as her mother must have told her. Why, if he had a pretty daughter like her, with such pretty hair, he, too, would forbid her to talk to strangers. As for him, he is hardly a stranger anymore, is he? They have what you might call broken bread together, he says, and laughs. Sidonia, too, laughs and licks the chocolate from the sides of her lips.

He draws himself up and repeats his name solemnly. He says he wants her to know he has been a navy man for many a year, that he trained in the navy as a young boy just out from England, that his life has been the navy, that he has known nothing but the sea and ships, and he looks down the glistening road as though it were the sea and the black limousine parked at a short distance from the cinema, a vessel in the night.

He adds, surely she is clever enough to be able to tell a villain from a hero?

Sidonia notices the slight swell of his stomach beneath his waistcoat and the creases in his khaki trousers. She hesitates because the man is not fair-haired and blue-eyed, after all, and she wonders if he will do.

Then she says that she knows someone who has even prettier hair.

He says, "You don't say. And where, may I ask, is this treasure to be found?"

Sidonia tells him that her friend is staying at the hotel with her. She adds that sometimes she and her friend turn on the lights in the hotel pool and go swimming naked at night like two goldfish in a bowl.

The man's dark eyes widen.

Sidonia says she is almost ten and that her friend is a little older.

The man says, "Ah, indeed," and touches her cheek and stares at her dreamily. He says that in his opinion almost ten is a perfect age, not too young and not too old, and there is nothing much wrong with a little older either.

The man says he would like the opportunity to compare Sidonia's pretty hair with her friend's, that very moment. But would her mother not be waiting up for her?

Sidonia runs her fingers through her hair. She says, "My mother never waits up for me. She has better things to do."

The man says that his ship is waiting to take them to her port, and grasps her hand.

The black limousine pulls up beside them. Sidonia says, "Why don't you come with me."

"With you?" The man asks with a start, dropping her hand. Sidonia says that her driver will take them both to the hotel, where he can meet her friend.

The man says, "Are you certain your mother will be asleep?" The driver is watching them through the window of the limousine. Sidonia laughs and says that the driver will not mind if there is another in his car.

Sidonia puts her head in the window and tells the driver that this nice naval captain wants to come to her hotel to meet her friend.

The Indian waiter gets out and walks around the car silently, only his starched white uniform rustling. He smiles at the man and says that Sidonia's friend is very lucky, as he predicted she would be. He looks at Sidonia and smiles sadly and says Sidonia's friend is very lucky to have Sidonia as a friend. Then he opens the car door for the man. He bows his turbaned head elegantly and says, "Welcome, Captain." The man steps in the back of the car.

Sidonia sits down beside him, her gaze meeting the driver's in the mirror.

PEACHES AND PLUMS

THE FATHER TOOK THE CHILDREN for long walks on Sundays because he imagined they shared his enthusiasm for the flat fields of the Beauce in summer, with the light clouds drifting across a pale sun, the hawthorn hedges flecked with fragile white flowers, and the edges of the wheat stained with red poppies. But the two girls did not share his enthusiasm for the flat fields of the Beauce, or even the sight of an occasional rabbit darting for cover, or the floppy brown ears of the pointer reappearing in the wheat. It was convenient for the father to imagine the girls shared his enthusiasms, but the truth was, all they shared was their name, Trubetskoi, which was embarrassingly difficult to pronounce, and the houses they lived in with their mother, and the Scottish nanny, and the cook from the Gold Coast. They lived in the winter in a house on a blind street in Paris, and in the summer in a villa on the side of a cliff in Italy, and then in the old stone mill in an unexpected declivity in the Beauce.

When the two girls lagged behind on the muddy fields, their father would wait impatiently for them to catch up and talk as he strode onward in an effort to entertain them. "The first time I met Pamela," he would say with a little tremolo in his voice, his eyes misty, speaking of their mother as though they had no connection with her, "she was standing at the door in the sunlight in the Parioli with a Panama hat in her hand. She looked like that Gainsborough—or is it a Reynolds portrait of Lady Hamilton? You know the one I mean, where she holds a straw hat in her hand with that flush in the cheeks and that russet hair tumbling down her back and the soft laughing mouth and that air of rushing in or out somewhere. She was Enrico's girl then, of course. You remember the Italian, don't you?—the one who was the papal guard. He'd taken me to see her, this girl he had found, who came from some wild country and, he said, had *tante di quelle miniere di diamanti*," and the father would imitate Enrico—whom the children had never heard of before—speaking Italian and shaking out his long slim fingers to indicate the gold mines or the gold or money, anyway, the children understood, falling from his fingers like leaves from a tree. The father would stare down at the girls expectantly, apparently waiting for some sort of response, a laugh, perhaps, but he seemed not to be seeing them, his two girls, Sarah and Anne, with their limp pigtails, their gray slanting eyes, and their cold pink knees, exposed in the kilts brought back from Edinburgh by the nanny and let down from the waist, so that they never seemed to grow out of them. The father seemed to be seeing imaginary children, boys, perhaps—their father had always wanted boys—red-cheeked, rambunctious boys who would run around the fields and chase rabbits, not pale-faced, frail girls who were frightened of big dogs and bored by these long monotonous walks and preferred to lie in their warm beds and eat chocolates and read books or sit by the fire and listen to their mother tell stories.

Their father spoke in cadences that seemed strange to the

girls, full of unfamiliar idioms, unlike their mother's or even their nanny's clipped formal English where the sentences were ordered and precise, with the adjectives and the adverbs in place. He did not seem to realize how odd he sounded or how strange he looked to the girls. Everything about their father seemed embarrassingly excessive: he had a large arched nose, a big mouth, and thick dark hair on his chest. He was very tall. He had long legs, long arms, a wide stride, and he swung his head from side to side like a metronome as he walked. They had to crane their necks to see his face, and when they saw it, which was not often that summer—he would appear suddenly on a Sunday morning sometimes, scattering the pebbles of the drive-way as he charged up to the house in his Porsche—he never looked the way they had imagined him. Nor did he correspond to their mother's description of him, which was handsome. Even the Scottish nanny, who obviously did not approve of their father, said he had a *certain presence*. Nor did he resemble his photographs, which their mother kept in prominent places, such as the piano in the drawing room. In the photographs, he was always wearing a wide-brimmed hat and grinning broadly, and he looked very pleased with himself; he rarely looked that way that summer. On the contrary, he seemed solemn and anxious, as though he were about to tell the girls something, but just not right away.

As for their mother, she tiptoed around the house silently in their father's presence like a shadow and hovered near the telephone in the hall in his absence, as though it were a volcano that might erupt at any moment. The traces of their mother's presence, when he was there, were always apologetic. She kept her voice low, and her clothes pale and soft. She lost weight, and even her lovely thick red hair seemed thinner and less red. All these changes told Sarah, the elder of the children, that her father was rather as frightening to her mother as he was to her.

Sarah believed her father did not care for his children particularly. This was not of great consequence, as they did not depend on their father in any practical way. Their mother provided for their well-being. She was a melancholy but steady presence. That summer she wept rather too copiously over *Little Women*. She seemed to the girls a failure as an adult.

Sarah could remember summers when the sun had seemed warmer and the old mill less damp and cold. This summer was so cold and damp that both girls wore their flannel shirts and their Shetland sweaters, although the wool pricked their necks. Despite the three years' difference in age, the girls were always dressed identically. They wore their long woolen socks, their heavy lace-up shoes, and their short kilts. As they tramped across the wet fields, thick mud clung to their shoes. Wind stung their knees. Their hands were bluish with cold. The sky was low, the clouds heavy as stones. They dragged their feet with difficulty, toiling along behind their father listlessly. The wheat was not as high as it should have been for that time of year, and if it rained again before the harvest, the farmer told them, the crops would be ruined.

Then the weather changed: the sun blazed fiercely in a white sky, and the leaves of the chestnut tree on the edge of the fields hung down heavily like ripe fruit. White dust blew up in their faces as they descended the narrow road that went past the local mansion with its high iron fence and slow swans reflected in dark still water. The mansion seemed smaller than Sarah remembered it. The garden had gone wild, the paths were overgrown. Sarah watched pink petals fall slowly to the ground.

"Apparently Mlle de Marcy has eloped with a Spaniard and left for Spain," their father told them, speaking of the owner of the mansion, as they pressed against the iron bars of the gate.

"What's eloped?" Sarah wanted to know.

"You know, run off, gone away, beat it," the father replied impatiently. He was always telling Sarah she asked questions to which she knew the answers, but it seemed to Sarah that there was always some piece of information that did not fit. It was a puzzle that she was unable to fit together.

"Why would she want to run off with a Spaniard?" Sarah asked, because she remembered Mlle de Marcy as an elderly lady with hair that stuck out like little gray wings on either side of her pale face. She wore a gray pleated skirt and a cardigan and pearls and had once come for tea with Sarah's mother and smoked a cigarette and tried to sell her mother a field.

"For God's sake, child, at your age, don't you know why women run off with men?" her father exclaimed.

Sarah did not believe babies were brought by the stork or found under cabbage leaves. Nor did she believe the magazine she had once read with pictures of men with whips and women in short leather skirts and no tops, their legs spread apart, draped in chains. She looked up at her father and tried to think of something appropriate to say, but he had already moved on, was striding down the road under the tall leaning elms, so that he seemed suddenly small and alone, even lonely. She wanted to call out something to him, but she was not sure how to call him back, or whether to call him Father, which sounded strange, or Michael, as her mother did, or even Mr. Trubetskoi, which everyone else in the house called him.

Sarah became aware of a monotonous, aggravating noise at her side. She looked up and saw her sister, who had left the road and was sitting on a log, kicking her shoes against the wood and wailing, "I'm tired of walking. I want to go home to Mummy." Her mouth looked large and red and ugly.

"Well, go home to Mummy, then, if you're going to be such a baby," Sarah said. Anne kept sucking her thumb.

"Go on, go home. I'll catch up with you in a minute,"

Sarah said, though she was not at all sure her sister could find the way home. Nor did she intend to catch up with her. She watched Anne walk alone down the road, aware that the trees had darkened, and the sky was swept clean of cloud. It was that time of day when the French sky turned brilliantly clear for a moment before the fall of night. Sarah felt the eyes of unseen animals, hares, squirrels, foxes, a lone wolf watching her from the woods, as her sister walked off uncertainly, her head bowed, wiping her cheeks with the back of her hand.

Sarah looked up at the mansion and a light glimmering in an upper window and imagined Mlle de Marcy and her dark-skinned Spaniard lying entwined in one another's arms on the floor. She shivered and then without a glance over her shoulder ran along the road under the leaning elms. She ran up the hill, her heart pounding, the glare of the setting sun in her eyes. She ran on toward her father. At first she thought he had disappeared, but she found him standing in the gloaming, gazing blankly at the dark roses climbing up the stone wall.

"Where's Anne?" he asked Sarah.

"Gone home," Sarah replied. Her father found this explanation satisfactory. She slipped her hand into his, and he looked down at her, as though he had just noticed her. He asked her to remind him just how old she was now, and was it not ten or eleven, a big girl in any case, and did she not know a thing or two? They walked on in silence while Sarah wondered what to respond to such a question. As night fell, her father told Sarah what she had already guessed. Anne, Sarah was certain, had fallen into a ditch in the dark by then. When Sarah asked him for some sort of additional information, her father thought for a moment and said, "You know, it's rather like having a plum and a peach on your plate, and not being sure which one you want to eat."

Sarah tried to imagine whether her mother was the plum

or the peach, but neither fruit resembled her mother's slim, pale shape. Sarah walked along the dust path in the dark, concentrating. What came to mind was the unknown woman. Sarah imagined her quite unlike Sarah's mother, quite unlike Sarah herself. She saw her as a woman who was courageous, who would never have deserted her little sister in the dark, or wept over Little Women, a woman with lustrous dark hair and flashing black eyes, big bosoms, and a plum-shaped behind, a woman who danced with a high comb in her hair, a woman called Candela, like that Spanish girl at school, who smoked cigarettes through a cigarette holder, and swilled red wine that stained the dark hair of her upper lip, and sat with her knees apart. Sarah imagined the woman with her father's baby, a plump, red-cheeked boy, slipping across bright satin on her rounded hip.

The moonless night was now dark. Above the great flat French fields, there were only a few pale stars. Sarah stumbled blindly along the dust road beside her father, her hand burning in his.

PART TWO

ADOLESCENCE

CRACKS

FIAMMA FAINTED IN CHAPEL THIS MORNING. The teachers do not know we make ourselves do it, though they suspect we do. They even had a doctor brought in to examine us, but he said there was nothing wrong with us. He said he had never seen such a healthy group of growing girls. We do look healthy. Our skins are gold with all the sunshine, and our hair and teeth look very white in contrast. Weekdays we wear short-sleeved white blouses and green tunics with their big Rs embroidered on our chests and our short green socks. Our tunics are worn four inches from the ground, measured kneeling, so you can see our knobby knees.

Perhaps Fiamma did not make herself faint. Perhaps she just fainted. The girls on the swimming team take turns fainting in chapel. We all know how to do it. Before Communion, while you are on your knees and have not had any breakfast, you breathe hard a few times, and then you hold your breath and close your eyes. You sweat and start to see diamonds in the dark. You feel yourself rush out of yourself, out and out. Then you come back to the squelch of Miss G's crepe shoes, as she strides along the blue-carpeted aisle to rescue you. She makes you put your head down between your knees, and then she lifts you up and squeezes your arm. Miss G is our swimming teacher, and she is super strong.

You lean against her as you go down the aisle and feel her breath on your cheek, and the soft swell of her boosie. Your heart flutters, and you see the light streaming in aslant through the narrow, stained-glass windows: red and blue and yellow like a rainbow.

Miss G leads you out into the cool of the garden. You sit on the whitewashed wall under the loquat tree in your white Sunday dress and undo the mother-of-pearl button at your neck. Miss G sits on the wall beside you and smokes a cigarette, holding it under her hand, so Miss Nieven, our headmistress, who has an M.A. from Oxford, will not notice if she comes upon her suddenly. When Miss G tells you to, you take off your panama hat and set it down on the wall. Then you lean your head against her shoulder. You get to sit there under the cool dark leaves of the loquat tree and feel the breeze lift the hem of your tunic very gently and watch Miss G blow smoke rings until she asks if you feel all right now. Her voice is deep and a little hoarse, like a man's.

Meg Donovan, who is a beauty and comes from Barbeton, says she thinks Fiamma might be preggie. Meg's mother often fainted when she was preggie. One time Meg saw her mother fall down from the table where she was turning around, having a hem pinned up. Meg has five sisters, and they are all at our school. She says her father says they should name a wing of our school after him because of all the tuition he has had to pay.

Di Radfield, whose thin lips dip at the corner ever since her father committed suicide in the bath, says Meg must be mad. Fiamma has not even got the curse, so how could she be preggie? Ann Lindt wonders who the father could be. There are no men around here except for the night watchman, John Mazaboko, and the servants, and Sir George's bones and those of his dog, Jock. Fuzzie who wants to be an opera singer like Mimi Coetzee, says, "Maybe you can do it to yourself in the dark if you cross your legs and rock the bed."

In our school the only snow we have at Christmas time is made from cotton wool, and the holly is made of plastic. It is so hot we sweat when we eat the roast turkey and the roast potatoes and the gem squash, and when they flame the Christmas pudding, the light outside is so bright you can hardly see the flame. The poem we read does not make much sense to us, as April is not the cruelest month and it breeds nothing out of the dead land.

Our school is surrounded by farmland. No one is here except the teachers, who are mostly spinsters from England, and the girls. The teachers clasp their hands to their hearts and look across the dun veld to the distant horizon and talk about the lilac in May. The girls loll in the leather chairs in the common room and talk about boys. They lie out on the lawn and listen to Elvis Presley singing "Nothin' but a houn' dog" on the gramophone. They sleep over sums in the classrooms or whisper in the library, as they pretend to look up Latin words. They move their mouths in silent prayer in the chapel and ask God, please, please, let Miss G choose me for the swimming team.

Near the school a few mangy cows graze, and mud huts stand, and wattle trees line the riverbanks, casting their thin shade. The river is hardly a river, just a few pools of dark, trapped water where the mozzies breed. Sometimes it does not rain for months. The earth cracks, and the soil strangles the roots of the flowers. The dust roads lie dry and white as shells, and in the afternoons when we walk, there is dust on our lace-up shoes. No fan-shaped sprinklers wave back and forth in the evenings to cool the air, and we are not allowed to take baths. The smell of sweat mingles with that of sweet dusting powder and Mum's deodorant and the 4711 that we splash behind our ears and pour down our fronts. Once the thatched roofs of the rondavels caught fire and the night watchman, John Mazaboko, had to come running with his hose.

The graves of Sir George Harrow and his faithful bullterrier, Jock, rest in the shade of a frangipani tree. The school once belonged to Sir George. There is a portrait of him in the library, wearing a monocle and looking old and dried out. Under his portrait it says he was a High Commissioner. The graves are out of bounds, but we sometimes run there to lie down on the cool marble slab and fold our hands on our chests and play dead.

Fuzzie was playing "All things bright and beautiful" loudly on the upright piano when Fiamma fainted. Fuzzie thumps when she plays the piano, and we make the gesture for an organ grinder behind her back. Even so, you could hear the dull thud when Fiamma's head hit the back of the pew. Then you could hear Miss G advancing down the aisle, her starched khaki jumpsuit rustling and her crepe-soled boots squelching, coming on valiantly, head held high, like a knight in armor. Miss G looked beautiful and brave, and the chapel looked like a castle. Fuzzie says Miss G has an *aquiline* nose, which means she looks like an eagle.

Miss G is lots of girls' crack. When you have a crack you see things more clearly: the thick dark of the shadows and transparence of the leaves in the light and the soft glow of the pink magnolia petals against the waxy leaves. You want to lie down alone in the dark in the music room and listen to Rachmaninoff and the summer rains rushing hard down the gutters. You leave notes for your crack in her mug next to her toothbrush on the shelf in the bathroom. If you accidentally brush up against your crack, and feel her boosie, you come close to fainting.

Sometimes Miss G calls the twelve of us on the swimming team into her room and tells us to shut the windows and shutters. We sit in the half-light and listen to her talk. She tells us to watch men in their bathing costumes, how they swell when they come near a girl. She makes us feel we are snake charmers. She says Miss Nieven is a lezzie with Miss Lacey, the English teacher, whom Yeats once loved. Miss G has seen them in the moonlight in Miss Lacey's square green Chevrolet.

Fiamma has misty gray eyes and pale freckles and thick dark hair. She walks very straight, as if her head were a crystal vase, she was balancing on her shoulders. Fiamma comes from the lake district in Italy, and she is the only girl in the school who is an R.C. They let her into our school, but she has to come to chapel with us. She lives in a big villa with many servants. She is supposed to be a princess or something like that, and before she arrived Miss Nieven told us to be polite and treat her kindly.

We learned about Bloody Mary in history and how she killed lots of people. She was an R.C. We read a poem by the greatest poet in the English language, according to Miss Lacey, and he asks God to avenge the saints slaughtered by the R.C.s. Perhaps Fiamma saw someone slaughtered, and she was thinking about it when she fainted in chapel. Perhaps that is why they have sent her away from her lovely villa, which is near a blue lake and mountains.

Fiamma has very white skin and suffers terribly from the mozzies. Fuzzie says Fiamma bathes in champagne to keep her skin so white. Di Radfield says it is milk. Maybe that is why it attracts the mozzies. Fiamma has big red welts on her calves and her arms. She spits on her mozzie bites and says the mozzies are eating her alive. Ann Lindt told her to use repellent, but

Fiamma says it stings too much.

Fuzzie says Fiamma fainted because someone gave her the Black Spot. The Black Spot frightened Fiamma because she believes in vendettas like all Italians. Fuzzie can sing "La Donna e mobile" from Rigoletto.

We torture all new girls. We make them eat bitter aloe or swallow cod-liver oil. Sheila Kohler tried to make a new girl put her head down the toilet, but the girl refused. Sheila Kohler said, "But you have to," but the girl just walked away.

Ann Lindt says she does not think Fiamma would have fainted because of the Black Spot. Ann Lindt knows everything. She reads *The Manchester Guardian*, which is sent to us from England on special thin airmail paper and pinned to the bulletin board, where it flaps about in the breeze that comes in through the open windows. Ann Lindt told us we were in danger of war over a crisis in the Suez Canal. She asked Miss Nieven why the natives do not have the vote. Miss Nieven said democracy takes a long time to develop.

Ann Lindt has to wear thick glasses because she is always reading. She reads books by Winston Churchill, who was attacked in an armored train in the Boer War. She sits in the window sill in the early morning before we get up and reads Winston Churchill's *Great Contemporaries* and looks up the words she does not know, words like *internecine* and *belligerent*. She says they do not read *Treasure Island* in Italy and so Fiamma would not even know that if someone gives you a piece of paper with a round blackened circle on it, it means they are going to kill you.

Most of us came here as boarders at five or six because there were no proper schools where we lived. We left our parents on distant farms or small towns. We traveled alone or in little groups for days on dusty trains through the dry veld. We arrived exhausted and confused, stumbling through the long, narrow dormitories, lit only by Matron's torch, and finding our beds among strange sleeping girls. The sheets smelled damp and funny. We lay awake listening to the dry wind clashing in the palm trees and tried to count the stars.

We cried for our mothers until Matron came and told us to be quiet, we would wake the other girls. When we got to the hiccupy stage she took our temperature with a thermometer that she keeps in a small glass of Dettol. Her name is Mrs. Looney, and we think she is, too.

Even now sometimes, we lie awake sniffing and hiccuping and imagining our mothers: they come to us in the half-dark, their soft breaths on our cheeks as they sing us familiar songs or recite rhymes we know: *She shall have music wherever she goes.*

At first we saw our mothers' faces as we tried to untangle the knots in our hair, or when we left our soap in the big bath with the feet in the bathroom under the stairs. We thought we heard our mothers calling our names, and we ran down into the bamboo at the end of the garden, catching glimpses of them parting the bamboo and stepping toward us in green silk dresses, but it was the cry of a sparrow hawk or the wind in the leaves.

We made up imaginary friends. Fuzzie's is called Margaret, which is her real name. We call her Fuzzie because of her curly hair. She runs around the hockey field until the breath rasps in her chest, talking to Margaret. At night in the dormitory Fuzzie tells us stories of Chinese girls who have blue eyes and blond hair, and Zulu maidens as pale as lilies. Ann Lindt interrupts and says such things are not possible. But we like to fall asleep to the sound of Fuzzie's voice. We feel ourselves spin out into the darkness, round and round, like a leaf on a lake.

Before she fainted in chapel this morning, Fiamma rose at dawn and went to swimming practice. Fiamma may be an R.C., but she is an excellent swimmer. Miss G says she can teach anyone to swim fast. All you have to do is to desire it. Miss G says desire is everything. We all like the way she says *desire*.

Miss G made us all race this year, now that we are in the senior school. She said we could choose any stroke we liked. She made us wait forever on the grass in our thin black costumes, while she strode up and down the edge of the pool with the yellow whistle in her mouth. Miss G's hair is glossy as a blackbird's and cropped so short you can see the bristles at the back. When she strides up and down you can see the shimmer of sweat on her strong arms and the dark shadow of the shaved hair between her strong, brown legs.

We felt the sun burning the skin on our shoulders puce. We licked powdered sugar from the flat of our palms for energy. Then Miss G called out our names and had us line up. Our legs felt watery, like the reflections of legs in water. We giggled and squirmed and pulled the straps of our green plastic caps away from our chins.

She lifted her black gun in the white air and fired. We hear the crack of the gun. Birds shot up in the air. We flung ourselves across the water for the two lengths. We splashed and kicked into one another. Fiamma left the rest of us behind after a few strokes. When Sheila Kohler saw she was not winning she threw her hands up in the air and sank down into the water.

Fiamma says her house is surrounded by regular gardens with gravel paths and ancient trees and a stone wall by the lake. She says the house is old and large and filled with flowers, and the cannas flame red and orange at the edge of the lawns. There are flowers in every room—roses and sweet peas and strelizias. There are lilies and peonies and baby's breath. There are flowers everywhere, she says—on every table and cabinet and inlaid chest, on every marble mantlepiece and even on the tops of bookcases. In the entrance hall there is a forest of flowers. Fiamma maintains the whole house looks like a hothouse.

She says there are many old paintings lit up with little lamps over the gold frames. Mostly, they are so dark you can hardly see the half-peeled fruit or bleeding hares. In one of the paintings she says there are two women staring at you, face-on, with a sort of dead expression. Their hair is done up high on their heads and their stiff boosies are bare. One of the women holds a nipple of the other gently between her long white finger and thumb.

Di Radfield says she woke up early, too, before chapel this morning and saw Fiamma hunting for her swimming costume. Fiamma is always losing things. She is used to having servants pick up her clothes from the marble floors of her big villa. Fiamma brushes her cheeks with a toothbrush every night before she goes to bed to make them glow. She adds an Alka Seltzer to the flat water to make it fizz. She curtsies when she shakes hands with a grown-up.

Miss G says that no one will tell us the truth about life, certainly not that bunch of spinsters who know nothing about it. She says, "Think of the water as your home. Learn to do without breath. Stay light." She tells us not to roll about or twist our shoulders or lift our heads too high in the water, but to suck a little air from the side of our mouths. She tells us not to make any splash, to slice silently through the water.

We all wore our panama hats and our white Sunday dresses with the mother-of-pearl buttons down the front for confirmation, because Miss Nieven said this was not a fashion show. When we were confirmed, we had to go to confession for the first and the last time in our lives. Sheila Kohler cried afterwards. She said she had told the minister she had read banned books, but she was not sorry, because they told the truth. Ann Lindt said Sheila Kohler was just trying to get Miss G's attention.

We know who has the curse and who does not because we play Truth in the dormitory at night. We put our hands into a pile and then pull them out. Someone sits on the sidelines and calls out Stop, and whoever has her hand at the bottom of the pile has to tell the truth. That's how we learned that Meg Donovan let a boy put his finger up her winkie. Di said she was jealous of Meg and followed her around for days like a dog. Di says we get the curse early because we live in such a hot country, but Fiamma is an aristocrat and they do not get the curse as early as commoners, because they have blue blood.

Di Radfield says she had finished swimming practice this morn-ing before anyone else arrived. She says she saw the whole thing. Miss G was at the swimming pool early, striding up and down the edge of the pool. Then Fiamma got out of the pool and did a perfect swallow dive from the high board, opening her arms on the rising sun and orange sky for Miss G.

Di Radfield says she remained silently in the shadows in the changing room, waiting to see what would happen. She watched Miss G follow Fiamma into the changing room, going toward Fiamma with the light behind her. Di could not see Fiamma's face, because her back was turned toward Di. Slowly Fiamma slipped her arms out of her swimming suit straps and folded down the top. She spread her arms out on either side and shook her shoulders in a sort of dance. Little drops of water fell onto the concrete floor from the tips of her fluttering fingers. She stepped out of her swimming suit. Di saw her naked back, the bare white shoulders, the damp skin, only the cool morning air clothing her. All the while Miss G was watching Fiamma, and her face looked red and wet, her mouth slightly open. Then Miss G moved toward Fiamma slowly, put her arms gently around her. Miss G lowered her dark head to Fiamma's boosie and sucked. Di could hear her sucking like a baby.

When they had finished, Fiamma floated out of the changing room, leaving the door open. Through the open door Di saw the grass shining white in the early morning light and the soft yellow flowers on the mimosa trees like snow on the thin branches. Di Radfield put on her tunic quickly and picked up her panama hat and ran down the bank toward the school.

Di Radfield says she wanted to cry, because Miss G has never even grabbed her boosie, but instead she decided to tell Miss Nieven what had happened.

At evensong in chapel Fuzzie plays "Now the day has ended / Night is drawing near" on the upright piano, but she gets stuck on the first two lines and plays them over and over. The odor of incense is in our nostrils. Our sunburned faces float like pink petals in the dim light. We are worn out with the sun and talking about Fiamma. It is the sad time on Sunday night, and we cannot recall our homes.

Miss Nieven rises for the sermon. Her shadow looms long and thin on the wall. She tells us Fiamma will have to stay in the san for a while, that the doctor has to check her out. She has sent Fiamma our good wishes, as she knows we would have wanted her to. She says that this is the sort of thing that happens when you behave in a foolish way. She reads "When I was a child I spake as a child. . ."

On our knees we watch Di Radfield flip her hair back from her face and breathe out hard. She holds her breath and closes her eyes. We look for Miss G, but we already know she is not there. We know what has happened to her and that she will not be back. Miss Nieven is coming to the end of the prayers, and Di's time is running out. She is beginning to sweat, and she turns pale, but we know she will not be able to slump sideways into the aisle. She will not see diamonds in the dark.

THE ORIGINAL

IT WAS HER MOTHER WHO NOTICED HIM on the platform. She said, "Did you see that handsome young man?" Pamela did not notice him, as there were so many other things to notice. It was as though the world were suddenly illuminated. Even the familiar things around her had acquired an exotic quality in that ancient place where the world had begun: the flowers in her mother's straw hat trembling in the breeze; her mother leaning forward, striding onward on thin ankles, her dress blown against her knees, the porter, staggering and wheezing under his load of pink suitcases, hat box and vanity case, all with her mother's initials and combination locks. Then they were in the *carrozza*, and the luggage was all piled higgledy-piggledy behind them, and Pamela was listening to the sound of the horses' hooves on the cobblestones and gazing up at the terra cotta façades of the venerable buildings and at the long-stemmed pine trees, like lollipops, she thought. She was saying the word *rondini*. She had just learned it—such a wonderful word for swallows, turning and turning in the blue Roman sky.

Later, at the Dante Alighieri school, she was not the one

41

to notice him. It was the German girl, the one with the long legs like a boy and the skin that seemed lit from within, whom Pamela had taken home to her mother, because, really, they were making the German girl work far too hard in the family where she was an *au pair*, it was the German girl who said, "What do you think of him?"

Pamela replied, "Of whom?" without even looking in the direction the German girl was looking, because the German girl was always looking at boys and whispering in Pamela's ear, "What do you think of him?" Besides, Pamela was looking at the marble busts all around the long narrow room and at the teacher, the woman who had such a pale face and that air of tragedy about her. She was wondering if the teacher had lost a lover or wasted her youth on some scoundrel and was doomed to dry spinsterhood. The teacher was intoning Dante with reverence, a little tremble in her voice and one hand on her flat breast. Pamela was listening to the words (they made her shiver a little) thinking of that dark, wild wood, though, of course, she was not in the middle of her life but just at the beginning. Still, she was listening to the Italian words about the shades, while the German girl was whispering urgently, "The American, over there, don't you see?—the blond one who has his feet on the chair, he's watching you."

Pamela glanced over at him for a moment and noticed the way the boy's dark gaze shifted from hers when she looked across the room.

"Don't you think he's handsome?" the German girl hissed in her ear.

Pamela concurred, because she wanted to hear Dante's words and because, of course, the boy was handsome, leaning back indolently in his chair. But the German girl went on, though the teacher was looking up and staring at her severely, saying behind her hand, "What do you think?" Pamela was nodding her head and listening as the teacher resumed, *I fear he may already be so far astray.*

Pamela was wondering where the teacher might have strayed: was it into some doomed love affair with a married man, or with another woman, perhaps, pale and tragic as the teacher herself?

She and the German girl were going to catch the bus, sauntering onward, hand in hand, with the warm afternoon sun on their shoulders, and Dante's words still ringing in Pamela's ears. She hardly heard him when he called out to them, and she would not have slowed her steps, had the German girl not tugged at her hand, so that he could catch up with them, coming on at a rapid pace on long legs and commenting on the teacher or the class or the grammar. She was listening to the sound of the water running in the shell-shaped fountain and staring at a lovely, solemn Madonna in a niche above it, her hands folded in prayer, a bunch of half-dead lilac at her chipped feet.

He told her he had seen them at the station, and that he had thought she looked like something out of a painting, a Venetian painting, because of her coloring, and that her mother resembled her—really it was quite uncanny the resemblance— that the mother looked like a copy, a pale copy of her. Then she stopped, laughing at the thought of her mother like a copy of anyone else. She said, "Surely, it's the other way round. I must be the copy, coming later, after all?" He would have none of that. Pamela saw her mother suddenly as a copy, though beautiful, of course—her mother had always told her what a great beauty she had been, that Pamela, though beautiful, would never be as beautiful as she.

The American asked if they would like to have a drink with him, a lemonade perhaps, here, and he was motioning to the cane tables and chairs on one side of the square. She stood looking across the wide square at the swallows turning and the fountain running and the dome of the Pantheon, housing the dead, arching vast and gray into the sky. The German girl was saying how hot it was, and how thirsty it made her.

The boy asked Pamela where she had come from. The German girl told him about Pamela's far-away home in a new country, about the jacarandas and the flame trees in the garden and the pet monkey. The boy asked Pamela, "Is it really like that?" Pamela explained how very hot it was at Christmas out there, and how cold in August, so that nothing corresponded to the words in the books she read, and how April was not the cruelest month at all, not breeding anything out of the dead land. She realized he must have asked something else, because the German girl was saying, "Well, do you think we should?" and staring at Pamela with her avid, brown eyes.

"I'd rather not," Pamela said, without knowing what he had asked.

"Why not? Have another drink," the boy was encouraging, and the waiter brought more tall glasses of fresh lemonade with those delicious sweet red cherries and long spoons. Pamela held the cold glass to her hot cheek and stared at a young girl in sneakers and seersucker shorts, who looked lonely and wrote postcards earnestly which Pamela was quite sure no one would ever read.

Pamela realized that what the boy had been asking them was to come home to supper with him, because the German girl was saying that they would have to let Pamela's mother know. Pamela shook her head and said her mother would be expecting them, though she knew her mother would not be expecting them, she would be sleeping as she did every afternoon in her bedroom, naked under the silk coverlet, sweating under her heavy hair, the curtains closed on the light. Perhaps she would already have dressed and strolled out into the garden, sipping the first of several drinks in the garden of the villa she had rented in the Parioli, at great cost, so that Pamela could learn the foreign languages her mother had never learned.

The boy told Pamela how he had told his mother all about her, about the pink suitcases and the flowers in the hats and about her mother looking so much like Pamela, except that her mother looked like a pale copy of Pamela, and how his mother had said Pamela sounded absolutely *dah-ling*, imitating his mother's Southern accent.

Pamela laughed and imagined his mother, a belle emerging from her wisteria-covered plantation house and drifting across blue grass, her father stabbed in the back by his jockey or kicked in the head by his horse. Pamela tried to rise and go, but the boy put his hand on her shoulder, saying, "No, please. Let's have dinner, at least."

The German girl said, "I am sure Pamela's mother would not mind if you come to dinner with us."

When they arrived at the villa in the Parioli with the sun setting and the glare in Pamela's eyes, Pamela stood watching her mother float across the lawn on her thin ankles, the breeze blowing the flowered dress against her body. Pamela could see the shape of her body beneath the flowers, and wished her mother's flowered dress were not cut so low and that her breasts were not so prominent. The German girl introduced the boy to her mother, who began moving her hands and talking to him about her last visit to America.

Her mother suggested they all sit outside, the evening being so splendid, Rome so delightful in April, was it not?—and why did they not sit in the garden under the pines and have a drink before dinner? Her mother told the German girl, rather too loudly, "To bring out drinks." Her mother always shouted at foreigners, putting all the verbs in the infinitive.

The boy sat in a deck chair between Pamela and her mother in the shadow of the pines, and the German girl sat on the grass and leaned her bare back against Pamela's knees, so that Pamela could smell her sweet perfume. Pamela's mother intoned like a hymn the list of cities she had visited in America. Pamela sat watching the pine trees arching toward one another as though trying to touch, and the fading light becoming a tender yellow, shining on the German girl's face.

Pamela's mother said, "But I see an empty glass. No one is taking care of my guest." The German girl rose but rather too slowly, as though her limbs had become heavy, and she turned up her chin oddly to one side and smiled ridiculously, Pamela thought.

Pamela shifted her gaze to the boy, just as her mother said, "I'll never forget arriving by boat in New York and seeing the Statue of Liberty for the first time. How my heart leaped!" Despite the encroaching shadows, Pamela noticed how the boy was leaning back indolently in his deck chair beside her mother, leaning his handsome head slightly to one side and tilting his chin toward her. Pamela noticed the contrasts in his face: the dark eyes and the light skin, the white shirt of some transparent stuff slightly open at the neck and the black plaited leather belt, the Roman sandals and the cream trousers. The long, slender limbs might almost have been a girl's. Pamela noticed that he was smiling at her mother with complicity, his dark eyes sparkling and his lips full. Her mother's beautiful beringed hand lay for a moment on his knee.

PART THREE

COURTSHIP AND MARRIAGE

AMBUSH

IT IS OCTOBER, WHAT THEY CALL SUICIDE MONTH. In the harsh light the bars on the train windows look black to her. She stares out at the dusty yellow bushes, the low thin trees. The leaves seem transparent and give no shade. The soil is like clay, the land flat and arid, the sky white. As the train goes further up country, the pale mud huts become even poorer; their skeletal frames are visible. The heat increases. When she pulls the window open, she is assailed by dust. The air is taut and dry. The train moves so slowly it seems continuously on the point of stopping. It stops at each small station and sometimes at no station at all, and for no apparent reason. At times it slides backward on its tracks.

In the crowded compartment there are no conversations. Passengers sit and sway, listening only to the intermittent buzzing of the flies. Someone breaks the stillness, exclaiming, "What a bloody country!"

She goes into the crowded, narrow corridor and stands pressed against the wall. She stares out the dusty, finger-marked window. In the bush she sees a man and a woman entwined on the ground, startled in the act of love.

At the border a tall guard in a khaki uniform, his high cheek bones decorated with deep cicatrices like a carved wooden mask, pulls back the door to the compartment and stands with his legs apart. His skin is a deep black. His eye-lashes curl back tightly toward his lids. His glance flicks back and forth over the passengers. He orders them outside, and they file out onto the platform. They stand in columns, men in one and women in the other, waiting, documents in hand. A thick-set black woman in uniform runs her hands across Alix's body slowly, patting between Alix's legs.

Mark's mother is waiting on the platform at the station. Alix shrinks from the intensity of her gaze. Like Mark, the mother has the wide-spaced blue-grey eyes, the silky pale hair, the high cheekbones and long limbs that make them the most beautiful people Alix has ever seen. Unlike her son, the mother has the pallor of those who have shunned the harsh light of the African bush. It was the bush that got her son, some nameless fever, the telegram had said.

"I am so glad you arrived before dark," the mother says now and reaches for Alix's suitcase, but someone else, a stranger says, "Allow me," and carries her suitcase to the car for her.

The wheels of the old Morris stir up the dust which pours in through the windows. The road narrows into two thin strips with high grass between them. The wall of foliage presses close, the spindly branches brushing the windows of the car with a rattle. Shadows ripple through the trees.

The mother drives confidently, her head erect. She has tied a scarf around it, but wisps of fine, pale hair escape from the faded silk. She asks Alix to light her a cigarette. Mark's mother has taped to the back of the cigarette box, a numbered list of groceries, penciled in a neat hand. The brown bags of groceries are in the back of the car. Alix passes the cigarette to the mother who puffs and waves distractedly to the naked black children, their bellies swollen with hunger, their big opaque eyes staring at her from the side of the road.

An iron pipe resting on two oil drums blocks their way. On the shoulder of the road dark forms stand still in the twilight. Tall young men stare at the car. They are wearing the faded blue shirts of the Youth League. They carry truncheons and slashers. Mark's mother winds down the window and says something sharp to one of them. He backs off smiling sheepishly. He speaks to the other men who laugh. He removes the bar and wishes Mark's mother a good evening in English. Alix waits for the old car to start. The starter cranks and grinds, but the engine only coughs, splutters, and dies, like a car in a gangster movie, Alix thinks.

Moving finally, Mark's mother explains, "Of course, there are rebels everywhere, but what this lot is looking for is to scare anyone who passes into supporting the League. We pay them off, and they let us alone."

Alix replies, "But you stay on?"

The mother shrugs and says, "Where else would I find this?" and nods in the direction of the house.

The house stands at the end of the dust road on the high ground. The gables are ashen in the fading light. One of the windows is lit by a kerosene lamp. Beyond the lawns the river slides by silently. Alix thinks the rambling house with its crumbling stucco, lit by the head lamps looks haunted. In the dim green light of the dashboard, the mother puts her hand on Alix's knee, and asks softly, "Are you getting over Mark, darling?"

Alix presses herself back against her seat. "Does one ever?"

"That's why I wanted you to come here," the mother says. "Don't put off your grief. It will only make it worse."

Alix looks at her.

The mother says, "Stephen is still here. I wanted you to come before he left. You will be someone young for him."

Alix remembers what Mark said about his elder brother, "Mother's pet: the perfect son from the get-go, made his bed at three, I was told; always top of the class; won all the prizes, Oxford at seventeen."

"I see," Alix says.

The mother cups the palm of her hand gently over Alix's cheek, a cool soft hand. Alix remembers Mark's words, "The hand of iron in the velvet glove."

On the veranda everything is still except for the insects. The veranda opens to the garden and to chance meetings, casual conversations, catnaps, even, the swing seat reminds Alix, to sudden wild love in the shade on hot afternoons. She leans against the back of a wicker chair to steady herself, as she looks across the lawn at the river in the last of the light.

The flame trees beckon. As she descends the steps, goes toward the trees, the light softens, passing from crystalline to liquid. She stares into the distance at the line where sky and earth meet.

She imagines the rebels advancing through the bush, from village to village. She hears the sound of drums rising in the distance beyond the river.

She hears voices on the veranda. Stephen is speaking to his mother, and she answers with asperity. Alix has never heard her use that tone, but she knew it lay there just beneath the lilt in her voice. Alix makes out, "It is the least you could do."

"Poor darling, you look as though you need a drink," the mother says now, coming toward Alix where she stands in the garden. She puts her arm around Alix's shoulder and leads her back up the steps onto the veranda. Docilely, Alix submits, bent under the weight of a tremendous fatigue. The mother has changed into a blue dress with a blue chiffon scarf that makes her eyes look blue. Alix admires the fine lines around her big clear eyes, her wide pale mouth, and the way she stands, very straight and slender. The mother says, "Stephen, what's the matter with you, can't you see she's dying of thirst?"

He picks up a drink from the silver tray and without turning around to face Alix, hands her the drink. He has pale elongated hands. She takes the drink from him and sips thirstily.

The brother is taller than Mark was and so much thinner, he seems friable like sandstone, she thinks. He has thinning hair, which he has combed back neatly from his forehead. He has the same prominent nose, the soft gray eyes as his brother. His mother puts her arm around his waist and leans her head girlishly on his shoulder as she says, "I've got to put up with him, don't I? He's all I've got left." Alix watches him move abruptly away. There is a moment of awkward silence. Then the mother says, "Drink up, darling. We are going to have your favorite dinner, roast beef and yorkshire and baked apples, and then we are going to tuck you in for an early night."

Alix nods, thinking, *I will not remember; I will not let you make me remember.* She is giddy from the thin air and from the alcohol on an empty stomach. The sky is a deep blue, festooned with garlands of stars. In the distance, beyond the glittering river she can see the pale huts glimmering and faint wisps of smoke rising in the air.

The young servant in khaki shorts and shirt who served the dinner uses a candle to lead her upstairs to her room. It is the room where she has always slept. It has a red polished floor and is lit with a kerosene lamp which gives off a familiar odor. In the flickering light the Shasta daisies on the dresser glow with a milky sheen. The white sheet on the double-bed is turned back, and a daisy lies on one of the pillows. She shudders as she remembers how she and Mark once found huge gray spiders under the bed.

Alix looks at the servant. He is tall, bony, and barefooted, with slanting eyes and high cheekbones and shiny skin. He has long lashes and a solemn mouth. He seems to be the only servant left, but she remembers his mother, the cook. "I believe your name's Maboko?" she says, but he leaves without replying.

She extinguishes the candle but keeps the lamp burning in the bathroom. When she lies down, the constant drumming seems louder. She thinks she hears the spiders crawling beneath her.

She hears a door slam and footsteps on the stairs, in the corridor. Her door opens quietly and someone enters. A shadow looms against the wall. In the half-dark, breathless, she feels Mark is there with her.

But it is his mother who says, "I saw the lamp in the bathroom and came to see if you were all right. You can't leave the lamp burning all night, you will asphyxiate yourself." She sits down on the bed and kisses Alix gently on the forehead, her lips cool and soft. Then she says, "I cannot tell you how grateful I am you came. Tomorrow you'll go riding as you used to."

In the morning, Alix is woken by the sunlight piercing the curtains like a blade. She wanders through the house and out into the garden, barefooted. The grass is dun, the zinnias and dahlias are strangled in cracked earth, and the ancient trees look wraith-like, their leaves too thin to provide shade. She shades her eyes with a hand and stares at the house, noticing, in the intense light, the fissures in the stucco of the walls.

She goes into the big shadowy kitchen. There is a smell of overripe papaw and oranges and of some other fruit she cannot identify. Fruit flies hover around the rotting fruit. She notices the water puddling by the ice box on the cracked red floor and the odor of rancid meat. Her eyes ache slightly from the dust, and she is sweating in her jeans.

Maboko offers her weak tea with milk and sugar in a tin mug and ladles out thick dark porridge into a bowl sprinkling it with brown sugar. He cuts open a pawpaw, scooping out the black seeds. She cannot eat much and tears come into her eyes.

She says, "I am sure there are big spiders under the bed in my room."

Maboko has his back to her at the counter, but he says, "They won't harm you. They are big but not the dangerous kind."

She says, "They might be dangerous, and anyway I don't like them."

He looks at her and inquires, "You were engaged to Mark, weren't you?" She nods. He says, "And now the Madame wants you to marry Mr. Stephen?" Alix catches her breath and turns her head to frown and glance angrily at him.

Stephen stands in his jodhpurs in the open kitchen doorway, his back to the light, pulling off his gloves finger by finger, carefully. He asks if she is ready to go riding. He sounds falsely cheerful, artificially full of energy. "Are you up for this?" he asks.

She has not ridden for some time. On her last visit she spent her mornings lounging in a negligee on the veranda. She sat and admired the view, and read up for the English class she teaches at the school where she was once a student, while Mark went down to the tobacco barns in his truck.

Still, Alix says curtly, "Of course. Let's go," thinking it is better to be going somewhere, anywhere at all.

Stephen looks at her and says, "You had better take a hat in this heat. I'll saddle the horses."

She runs up the stairs and stands on the threshold of her room.

She sees the spiders, several enormous spiders on long hairy gray legs in the shadows of a corner of her room. She can hardly believe the size or the number of them. She tiptoes backwards, her hand to her mouth, about to call out. Instead she remembers the broom closet at the end of the hall. She runs down the hall. She goes back into the room with the broom handle held high. She beats the handle of the broom again and again against the spiders and the polished red floor. She goes on beating, shutting her eyes, unable to look, banging the wood against the floor, hearing the sound of the beating of the wood against the floor.

"They are quite harmless, you know," Stephen says. Then he asks, "Are you all right?" She nods. She has forgotten the hat, and she keeps her arms folded over her shaking hands.

The horse he has saddled for her is the black mare she has always ridden. Once it bolted with her, and Mark and his mother were obliged to rescue her.

There is no one on the road. A chicken squawks as it picks its way across. They walk the horses side by side in silence along a narrow dust path into the bush. A bird rises with a sudden dry sound of beating wings, and she fears her horse will bolt, but it does not. The beast, too, is beginning to age. They continue slowly, avoiding dongas, the deep scars that mark that place, going further and further into the wilderness, up and down stony hills, past baobabs, their huge trunks looking monstrous and distorted.

They come to the bank of the great river overhung with yellow fever trees. Looking down she can see the wide, dark fast-moving water. She leans forward to stroke the damp neck of the horse. She looks up into the branches of a tree and sees a *boom slang* slither away along a branch.

Stephen turns to her and suggests they rest by the river for a while. Politely he offers her his hand. She is glad to let him help her descend the bank. His fingers are dry and long and steady. Her legs feel like reflections of legs, watery. He finds a place in the shade and spreads a blanket on the bank. He gives her lemonade. He sits beside her, and she glances at his handsome face. The skin is as smooth as a mask. He stretches out beside her, propping his head on one hand and holding forth about the farm: the fences, the barns, the falling tobacco prices, the need for new machinery, the advances of the rebels. He uses the initials of the different groups, and he mumbles slightly, so that Alix has difficulty sorting them out. She imagines he is habitually silent but bursts forth in this way from time to time, his talk used not so much to communicate, as to stop her from talking. Finally he pauses and turns to her. He says, "Mother was hoping, of course, that you and Mark would stay here to help her with the farm. Actually, she has never wanted me to leave, either. There was someone once, but it didn't work out."

Alix says, "I'm so sorry," and puts her hand on his arm with sympathy.

Stephen says, "Don't tell Mother. She'll pump you, you know."

Alix says, "Why did your Mother ask me here?"

He whispers, as though his mother were listening, "But don't you know?" Then, after a moment, he asks, "Why did you come?"

"I wanted to see her, and I knew that if I did not come now, I never would. I kept putting it off, and then..." She gestures toward the trees, the river, a kingfisher swooping down for its prey sending up a flash of rainbow spray in the air. She adds, "The house, the beautiful house," and looks into his eyes. He looks away.

He says nervously, "We ought to get back to the house before dark. The rebels are all over the place. We should eat now. Mother had a picnic packed for us. You and Mark used to come here for picnics, she said?"

Alix suddenly remembers the night they camped by the river and how an anteater had scratched at their tent, and she had thought it was a lion. Mark had laughed at her, thrown her legs over her head and made love to her in the tent. Later they found the anteater had stolen their eggs.

She says, "I am not hungry now, thank you." Because the mother has packed food, is she obliged to eat it? She wonders what else the mother told the son to do.

She props her head up against the log and stares at the sky. He says, "I am going to eat," and she watches as he unwraps a sandwich carefully and takes a bite. He eats the entire sandwich fast with small methodical bites, drinks thirstily from the thermos, and wipes the top. He folds the wax paper into small squares and puts it into the brown paper bag; he screws the top on the thermos tightly. She can imagine him fussing over a speck of dust on the floor.

When he has put away the picnic and wiped his mouth carefully, he turns to her, says, "You know, I am very sorry about Mark."

She closes her eyes.

Stephen says, "He was so very much in love with you."

She puts her hand to her eyes, says quickly, "I know. I know."

He says, "He was always talking about you. He was so proud of you. He always said you knew more words than anyone else."

"Please, *please*," she says. She feels Mark there sitting beside his brother, watching them in the shadows. She is not sure if it is the shadow on his face, or if he is smiling at them. He reaches out to her: she can feel his hand on her arm. She opens her eyes, and watches herself lean over and kiss Stephen hard on the mouth. He shuts his eyes but does not return the kiss. She smiles at his expression of bewilderment, fear, and passive expectancy. She pats the ground beside her, and when Stephen does not move closer to her, she moves closer to him. He lies beside her on his back, hands behind his head, looking up at the sky, his bland handsome face expressionless, as though it were he who had died and not his brother. His stillness, his passivity excites her. And something else. All the while she is removing her clothes, touching his face, his chest, his legs, stimulating the slack slug of his sex, Mark is there watching her.

Afterward she thinks, *I am not in love with Mark, I am not in love with his mother, I am not in love with anyone at all.*

She lies in a bath of hot water. She dresses. Her knees tremble as she descends the stairs. She finds the mother waiting in the lounge. It is a big room that runs the length of the house with glass doors that open onto the veranda. Big bowls of white roses and freesias perfume the room. The fine old pieces of English furniture shine, the silver reflected in the dark wood. Cut-glass decanters shimmer on a silver tray.

The mother wears a starched white dress, close-fitting to the waist. The full skirt rustles as she floats across the polished parquet. Alix thinks of reading somewhere that queens wear white for mourning. The mother has washed her pale hair, and it shines brightly in the light. She looks fresh, rested, lovelier than ever. Her perfume mingles with that of the flowers.

"Brava, brava! Absolutely splendid, darling," she exclaims, clapping her hands, her face glowing, as Alix descends the stairs slowly. She gives Alix a drink, and tells her to sit beside her on the silk sofa, leans close to her. She says Stephen has told her how well Alix managed her horse. She says she should not have worried; she knew what a good rider Alix was, how capable she was, but they had come back so late, and she was so afraid something had happened. The mother says she cannot help worrying these days. The violence is getting worse. Every day there are reports of new rebel victories. It is not safe for a woman to go out on her own. She lowers her dark lashes and bites her lip. She says she has come to the conclusion that life is simply a process of loss rather like the song they used to sing as children in the car about the green bottles. She says, with a little tremble in her voice, that she is down to her last green bottle.

Alix thinks she does not look in the slightest bit sad, but rather as if she has lain in her bed and slept all day, rising late in the afternoon to fill the vases with armfuls of flowers from the cutting garden. Alix imagines her propped up high on white pillows in a loose silk gown, reading, raising her gaze from her book, her glasses perched on her nose, to tell Maboko to polish the furniture, and then rising to run a bath, pouring in oils, lying in scented water.

She takes Alix's hand and strokes her cheek and says she is so glad Alix is safe. She pours her another drink. Alix's head spins.

The mother asks her if Stephen has said anything about leaving. Alix looks at her blankly and shakes her head. The mother leans closer and removes something from the tip of her tongue. She says, "Come on, darling. He did talk about it, didn't he? I know he wants to leave. Tell me the truth."

Alix says, "You must let him leave. And I am going, too. I am glad I came, but I cannot stay. You must understand that. I have to get back to my work, my students, you know."

"What makes it difficult to live in this place makes it a good place to work. There is so much work to be done here. It would be such a challenge. They need good teachers more here than anywhere else," the mother says and touches Alix's hand, bringing her face close, so that the eyes seem very large.

The mother rises and goes over to a bowl of flowers. She lifts the white roses and the freesias from the vase, shaking the stems slightly to let the water fall. "I don't know if you're up for this, but perhaps you would like to come with me?" she asks Alix.

Alix looks at her and shakes her head slightly in query, although she guesses what the mother has in mind.

"It's very lovely in the moonlight. But you don't have to darling. I understand."

Alix catches her breath. She rises and says, "But of course. Allow me," and she opens her arms out. The mother relinquishes the flowers.

Garlands of stars dip across the black sky. They walk along the river. The water is white in the moonlight. The heat has retreated slightly but still lingers on in the night air. The thorns on the roses press into Alix's skin, and she shifts the flowers to carry them more easily. The mother, as though she has gathered a source of secret strength, surges ahead, but Alix hangs back stumbling after her, half blind.

The mother climbs the small hill fast, the heat increasing as they go along, so that Alix wants to call out, to tell her she cannot possibly accompany her, she has changed her mind. At the top of the hill Alix sees everything shimmer in the moonlight. There is not a sound except the mother's soft breath.

In the gloaming Alix makes out other stone family graves under the trees, and even the small grave of one of the family's favorite dogs. She stares at the mound of raw red earth and the white wooden cross with the name. In the night air the scent of the roses and freesias and the mother's perfume rises. She feels her heart flutter and then seem to stop. The word rises to her lips, perhaps she has even said it aloud. Dearest. She kneels to lay the flowers on the mound, and the mother kneels close beside her.

Alix murmurs, "There is nothing I can do to help, even if I wanted to. You must realize that, surely."

The mother says nothing, but simply gathers Alix into her arms and holds her close with a welcoming gesture, as if she had just arrived.

THE BRIDE'S SECRET

"Happy, darling?" he says.

"Oh so happy," she replies and throws her arms around his neck. He places his hands on her shoulders and looks down at her. She looks at his sensuous lips, his light eyes. They are a dusty blue gray, set close in his handsome face. He draws the palm of his slender hand over his broad brow and thinning hair. She takes off her high-heeled shoes, tiptoes across the thick, soft carpet, and touches the blue bedspread and curtains. She goes into the bathroom and turns on the lights. "Come and see: lemony lilies in a hotel bathroom!" she calls out.

When he does not reply, she returns to the room. He has drawn back the curtains and is looking out the window at the Place de la Concorde. He has opened the window, and a slight warm breeze stirs the voile under the curtains. It is early dawn; the sky glimmers white. The ancient stones emerge slowly from the mist, glistening damply. She stands beside him and looks at his hands lying on the window sill. They hold her attention—white, clean, limp. He looks out the window and says, "This is where the women sat and knitted while they guillotined the aristocracy."

She asks, "Are you all right? You are trembling."

He puts his arm around her and says, "It has been a long night. All those relatives, darling. You have just too many of them."

She laughs and snuggles against him. She says, "And all of them saying what a lucky man you are." She looks at him shyly from the side of her eyes.

She was sweating so heavily she could feel the trickle down her legs and beneath the white satin dress with the mother-of-pearl buttons and the heavy satin train. She stood in the open doorway of the hot, crowded church, the smiling faces turned toward her expectantly, the women in large elaborate hats and bright dresses, the men in dark suits, their hair glistening.

She sits down on the bed and strokes the light silk bedspread gently. She pushes her dark hair away from her face and asks, "Wouldn't you rather rest before we go out? You hardly slept on the plane."

He replies quickly, "Not on your life. Your first day in Paris." He glances around the room with its high ceiling and intricate moldings, its chandelier of tinkling tear-shaped glass. He paces. He seems to push aside the walls, to dismiss the objects that surround the two of them, wipe out the boundaries.

He goes on, "I am going to take you to a place I know. We'll order oysters and a bottle of champagne for breakfast. Then we'll sleep." He raises his thin eyebrows at her row of fat pink suitcases, all with her initials, their combination locks, their first-class labels. "You unpack, that will take you a while. I need a shower," he says, scratching his head and watching the confetti fall from his hair. He takes out his worn black leather shaving kit and snaps it open. She sees him pull out his razor and his shaving brush. Then he closes and locks the bathroom door behind him.

She lays her dresses out on the big double bed and looks at them, touching the materials. There is a black velvet dress with a full skirt for the opera, a light blue linen one with a V neck and buttons down the front, a narrow red cotton one with polka dots and a flounce around the hem. She hangs them up along with the fur wrap her mother insisted on, because occasions could be formal in Paris, even in the fifties. She spreads the long white nightgown across the silk counterpane. She pulls in the waist and folds in the narrow sleeves across the bodice like someone hugging herself. She places a pile of silk lingerie in the top drawer of the dresser, letting her hand linger on the white brassieres. She takes off her creased mauve linen going-away suit.

She stands before the mirror in her brassiere and half-petticoat. She turns sideways. The fullness of her breasts seem unfamiliar and burdensome. She hears the water running and, outside, the cars and buses rumbling across the wet square. It is not cold, so she puts on the blue dress and brushes her thick black hair and watches how it sways around her flushed face. Her skin glows. She smoothes foundation cream across the faint freckles on her nose. She pats powder on her flushed cheeks. She applies a glossy red to her lips and sprays perfume down the front of her dress. Outlined in blue, her eyes look violet and glitter wildly. If her eyes had been bigger and her thighs longer, she would have been beautiful.

She can still hear the water running. She sits on the bed. She should have brought a book. She had not thought to bring a book on her honeymoon. She leans back against the big pillows and closes her eyes.

She wakes with a start. He is standing over her wearing his black polo shirt, his hair wet and combed from his high brow. He is staring at her strangely, holding his razor and his shaving brush in his pale hands.

The saleswoman's hands were cold and trembled slightly as she adjusted the straps of the lace brassiere. She wore a black dress with a white pique collar and a pink pincushion on an elastic around her bony arm. She smelled of sweet, cheap dusting powder, and she had dark hair on her upper lip. There were large mirrors front and back.

The saleswoman said primly, "I do hope you won't mind my saying this, but I could not help noticing your beautiful breasts."

The leaves throb like hearts. A bell tolls the hour. A bird lifts and wheels in the white air as they cross the Place de la Concorde. The mist rises from the river. The tenderness of Paris mounts slowly like the rising sun. She stands in his shadow in her white beret and white shoes, leaning against the stone wall, listening to the voluptuous sound of the water. They cross the bridge and follow the quais. A black poodle zigzags along the street following a scent.

He says, "I am taking you to the *quartier* where I used to live. I want you to see all of the places where I used to go."

She asks, "Even where you went with other women?"

They walk hand in hand. He walks with long strides, his head slightly bent as if to conceal his height. She hurries in her high heels. A few drops fall. They take shelter under an arcade. He holds his tweed jacket over their heads.

The restaurant is almost empty. Waiters in white aprons over black trousers stand about with bowed heads. A few customers sit at the bar sipping vin rouge, motionless as statues in a public square. The wooden tables gleam.

The headwaiter walks fast toward them and shakes the hand of her husband, who introduces his bride. The headwaiter says something complimentary, she gathers. He keeps shaking his head at her husband and smiling and waving his plump hands.

He ushers them out onto the terrace. The rain has stopped, and the sun comes and goes behind drifting clouds. The air is warm, slightly steamy. They sit opposite each another in the corner under the thick green creeper.

The oysters arrive, plump, gray and pink, lustrous in their pearly shells, lying on a bed of dark seaweed on a silver pedestal. The black bread rests between the folds of a white napkin, and there is a little brown pot brimful with butter. She squeezes lemon on the oysters and slurps the soft flesh.

Her mother kissed her good-bye, held her close, and whispered, "Have a good rest, darling. Stay in and order room service, lots of room service," and slipped a thick wad of traveler's checks into her hand.

The bride turned to go. Her mother looked at her, held onto her hand and added, "There are some things best not known till after."

She watches his hands lying motionless by his plate. They look dead, pale, and rigid, like hands of plaster. She urges him to eat, but he only picks at the oysters, lifting them up to the light, then setting them down. She starts to eat his. He continues to sip champagne.

She says, "I want to hear all about the women you knew back then." He laughs, looks at her with his pale hooded eyes and continues to sip his champagne. She wants to ask him why he never married any of them.

His mother stepped out of the dark stone church into the harsh glare of light and gathered her into her arms with an almost boneless movement, compressing a heavy Victorian brooch against her neck. His mother whispered to her, "I have always wanted a daughter, darling, and I cannot think of one I would want more. You will bring him what he lacks. You're going to take him in hand now. It is all up to you."

The headwaiter returns to continue the conversation. She nods as though she understands, but she feels very sleepy, half-drugged, and the muscles around her mouth are stiff from forced smiling. From time to time she touches her husband's hand, asks him what he is saying, but he only shakes his head and smiles distractedly. Finally, she finishes the oysters and goes to the bathroom.

The walls are papered a soft pink and there are two little stools with full pink skirts exactly like the ones at home. There are real linen towels threaded through a wooden stand so that no one can steal them. She sits before the mirror and brushes her hair, powders her cheeks, and rouges her lips. She remains there with her hands in her lap, staring into the mirror.

When she returns, her husband is talking to a woman in high heels and a tight-fitting cream suit, the large collar folded back like two giant petals and plunging low to reveal her rounded breasts. He introduces his bride to the woman, who appraises her carefully. The woman is commenting on her youth. She says something about cradle snatching in the colonies, and about the bride's round baby face. The woman inquires if she speaks French.

The woman's little white dog, with its red jeweled collar, jumps up on its hind legs and yaps. Called to order, he sinks obediently under his mistress's chair. The woman coos and mumbles alternately with care and evident coquetry. Heavily powdered, her lips thick and glossy, she has a dark beauty spot at the corner of her mouth. She drinks a *menthe verte*, the color of her large, penetrating eyes.

She lifts the bride's ring hand and says something to the husband about his extravagance, and he replies that the ring belonged to his bride's mother.

The bride says, "I am so tired, darling. I would like to go back to the hotel."

He says, "Of course," and he leans toward the woman. They confer seriously in low tones. The woman rises and waves a green gloved hand and vanishes with a swish of the revolving door.

He explains, "She used to teach with me. Also eighteenth century. She looks rather eighteenth century, don't you think? She tells me she has found some of de Sade's letters. They were written from jail, you know. When he wasn't in jail, he was too busy fornicating to write letters. Of course, many of them may not be interesting. Probably written to creditors, that sort of thing."

She says, "Do you plan to buy them?"

"I don't have that kind of money, but I would like to look at them. I can probably find her an American buyer."

She says, "I hope you are not going to spend your honeymoon reading the letters of the Marquis de Sade."

He laughs and says, "I would like to see her again before we leave. I don't know when I'll be over here again."

She says, "Yes, yes. I am beginning to feel eighteenth century myself. Can we go back to the hotel now? I am terribly tired."

When the waiter arrives with the bill, she opens her handbag and hunts for the thick wad of traveler's checks. Her husband puts his hand on hers. "Your mother has already been generous enough. This is my treat, darling."

She was carrying the heavy bouquet of lilies down the interminable aisle, the long satin train dragging behind her, the organ thundering, the incense rising in thick clouds, and the blue-and-red stained glass windows smoldering. She felt light-headed.

Her uncle strode beside her in his black tails and white carnation, his eyes very blue and his skin sunburned from days on the beach, toeing out and slightly flat-footed, flashing his friable white teeth, the sweet, spoiled child's smile, winking at the women. Then there was silence, complete and terrible as in a dream, while she stood at the altar sweating and sniffing, the tears falling across her powdered cheeks.

Out in the street she wants to hail a taxi, but he insists they walk along the street where he lived for several years. She stands in the shadow of the horse chestnut trees and looks at the small house with its dirty windows and iron bars. There is a dark wooden door, its green paint peeling, and its bronze knocker so worn it has lost its shape.

They walk in the Luxembourg Gardens. He shows her a tree with heart-shaped yellow leaves. She thinks it would be perfect for children to climb if they were allowed on the grass. She stares at the solemn little French girls in their long smocked dresses and high white socks, riding fat, slow ponies up and down the dust paths, and the little French boys in sailor suits, sailing boats on the fish pond. A sprinkler turns, the fine spray catching the light to form a rainbow. Her husband points out the neat beds of orange cannas and red impatiens and pink petunias arranged in fleur de lys patterns. She thinks the colors of the flowers clash. She does not like formal arrangements of flowers; she feels constrained by grass on which she is forbidden to walk. She says, "There are no butterflies in this garden."

She thinks of the wide bed at the hotel. She wants to take off her shoes, her lined dress, her beret, which now cuts into her forehead. She feels hot and light-headed. She leans on his arm heavily. They linger in the shade under the potted palms. She sits down, and an elderly woman in black appears and asks them to pay for their chairs. She feels a cramp in her stomach and a rising wave of nausea. "Please take me back to the hotel," she says, the saliva rising in her mouth.

She locks the bathroom door and kneels down on the floor. She vomits violently, then lies flat, the cramps running through her body, the lemony lilies swimming before her eyes.

She was standing on a table in the white satin wedding gown, turning slowly. The room was hot, and there was a fly stuck and buzzing in the sugar at the bottom of a teacup. Madame Vlamos, the Greek dressmaker, offered her Greek sweetmeats dusted with icing sugar. "Have another one, dear. Do have another."

"Oh, I really can't, really, I can't, " she said, feeling the wave of nausea rise, standing on the table in the white dress, watching her mother, who sat in her black-and-white checked suit turning the pages of a fashion magazine, slowly, one by one, not licking her finger.

"Keep turning dear, turn slowly now," Madame Vlamos mumbled, her mouth full of pins.

She wakes with a start. She looks around the dimly lit room. Her husband must have placed her on the bed, but he is not there. Everything is in order. She can smell the slightly cloying smell of the lilies mingled with his cologne. She returns to the bathroom opens the medicine cabinet, and sees the razor on the shelf.

She takes it out and touches the blade. She splashes cold water on her cheeks and drinks from the tap. She brushes her teeth. She runs a bath. She undresses and stands sideways and looks at her stomach in the mirror. She ties her hair up and lies back in the tepid water. She scrubs her body carefully and rises, the water running from her soft white body in silver cords. She wraps herself in a thick white towel and pads back into the room. She opens the curtains and lets in the bright late-afternoon light. It is the time of day when the French sky suddenly clears, just before the fall of night. She finds a note on the dresser that reads, "Have a good, long rest. Back soon."

She drinks thirstily from a bottle of mineral water and then lies down to wait. Put on your dress and go after him, she thinks, but she cannot; her head is still spinning. She listens for footsteps, for the action of a key in the lock. She slips her fingers into the cup of her lace brassiere and strokes her thick dark nipple. She closes her eyes.

She dreams. She hears footsteps on the veranda, a tapping on the wooden floor. A tall man stands menacingly over her bed. She cannot distinguish his features because he wears a stocking pulled over his head. He has a razor in one hand as he reaches for her throat with the other.

When she awakens again, the room is nearly dark. She rises unsteadily, puts on the blue dress, and picks up her handbag. She takes the elevator and walks out into the square. She watches the Parisian night seize the statues, the black walls, the quais and the bridges, all of them vanishing as though never to reappear. Long gleams of light wane in the monotone sky.

She could hear the sound of waves and the sea wind. It was hot, the sky the color of ash. The sun baked the dry dusty streets and penetrated the bamboo and the creeper-covered awning. The nuns had let the girls out early that afternoon, and she was reading her book in the fan-shaped wicker chair, sitting beside the potted fern with the feathery leaves in her shorts and sleeveless shirt, her bare feet propped on the wicker table beside the old yellow magazines and a pitcher of lemonade, the ice melting fast. She sipped the lemonade and crunched the ice with her back teeth.

Her uncle was smoking in the shadows and slapping his cheeks from time to time, his panama hat pulled down low and his legs crossed at the ankle. The tips of his fingers were stained yellow, and his hands shook.

Her mother slept on her back in the cool of her shuttered bedroom, her mouth slightly open, one arm flung across her face.

Her uncle said, "Stop doing that with the ice, will you? You are ruining your teeth." She turned the page. Her uncle said, "What about a walk on the beach?"

She said, "Too hot," and went on reading at the part where Mr. Rochester arrives in the dark and falls from his horse.

The soft, damp air blows on her face. The lights splash the wet square. A boat, garlanded with colored lights, passes under the bridge. She is bare-headed. Her raincoat is tied tightly at her waist. The rain falls like a veil between her and the city. She looks for him in the crowded streets where they passed that morning. A voice in her head records her actions, as though she is watching herself from outside. She thinks she sees the same stray black dog zigzagging along the street.

She goes into the place where they breakfasted. The main dining room is crowded. The headwaiter is red-faced and distracted. She tries to explain that she is looking for her husband, but he does not seem to understand. He ushers her out onto the terrace to a small table in a corner. She feels everyone stare at her, and she flushes. She orders a glass of mineral water and goes out again into the rain.

She wanders aimlessly down the Rue de Tournon, looking into the elegant shop windows. The rain starts to fall hard again; dark umbrellas bloom. Everyone passes her with bored expressions. She wonders why the Parisians look so bored. She sees a pink china cup and saucer with a gold rim in a shop window.

The shop is still lit, and someone is moving about inside. The bells tinkle gaily as she enters. There are Oriental carpets on the floor and precious objects on tables and in glass cases.

A short, plump man in a well-tailored suit approaches. He asks if he may help. She finds herself saying something about a present for her mother. The man asks in English what she would like to spend. She tells him that the price is not important. He laughs. She chooses the pink cup and saucer. He says, "You have very good taste, Mademoiselle," and his dark eyes glow warmly. She looks at the slight comfortable swell of his stomach beneath his waistcoat.

She picks up various objects, feeling his gaze on her. She draws herself up and swings her hips. She turns and smiles. He is standing behind her. She looks at his smooth skin and prosperous, florid cheeks.

He shows her an enameled pillbox. He presses on one side, and the lid swings up to reveal an octagonal mirror. He snaps the lid closed, and for a moment, she feels the pressure of his blunt-tipped fingers in her proffered palm. "It's perfectly lovely," she says, holding the pillbox in her hands. "It's smooth as butter." She examines the mirror and catches a glimpse of her face. She is surprised to see her plump lips smiling and peaceful. She pays, and the man wraps the pillbox in pink tissue paper and drops it, too, into the glossy white packet. His nails are beautifully manicured.

She has the impression the man knows all about her. She thinks he would not be surprised if she were to tell him that she was just out of boarding school, that this was her first time in Paris, her first time away from home, that this was the first night of her honeymoon, that she had lost her husband, and that she would like the man to take her somewhere for a drink. She imagines sitting in a small candle lit place on the Left Bank, talking with him about antiques. She would tell him about the old man who came once a week to wind all the clocks in their house, and how she would sit on the stairs in the dark, listening to the clocks chiming and her uncle's stertorous breathing. But she does not say any of this, and the man only goes on smiling.

On the street again, she walks in the shadow of the Louvre. The great building goes on endlessly. She thinks of the neglected prince who almost drowned in a fish pond here and later became the famous Sun King. The pavement seems very hard. Her new shoes hurt. She clutches her packet to her chest.

Her mother shut the door behind her, drew the curtains, and sat down, crossing her slim stockinged legs. Her mother said, "Sit down, dear, I have a suggestion. I'll let you decide. It's your life, after all."

She sat on the cool chintz couch and ran her finger around the silver ashtray with the little bird in the center, waiting.

Her mother said, "He's quite brilliant, has read everything you can think of, won all sorts of prizes, and speaks several languages. He plays the clarinet or the oboe," his mother said. "And he's very aristocratic."

"Aristocratic?"

"Well, he may even be a baron, something like that. At any rate he is a gentleman. He has lovely manners. You are too young to understand how important lovely manners can be, but in the end lovely manners are what count in life."

"But I hardly know him, Mother. He's very polite, as you say, but he doesn't seem very interested in me."

Her mother waved her beringed hand in the air. "You're so young. And he adores his mother. Such an intelligent woman, his mother. I liked her so much. She's very wise, the way only Frenchwomen can be."

"My studies? The university?"

"There is no need for you to study. What for? I am sure he will be good to you, darling. Besides, it's always the alternative that counts, isn't it?"

"What is the alternative?"

Her mother said, "You must know: to go to Europe quietly with one of your aunts."

She takes the elevator, mounting slowly behind the iron bars. She hesitates at the door. She tries the handle. She enters and finds him standing by the window. "I went to look for you." she says.

"Did you think I had abandoned my bride on her wedding night?"

She says, "I thought something might have happened to you," and throws her arms around his neck and holds on to him for a long while. He bends down and kisses the top of her head. She can smell the alcohol on his breath. He says, "That'll teach you to eat all my oysters. Are you feeling better?"

He walks over to the bed and switches on the bedside lamp. He says, "I thought you would be sleeping."

"I'm not used to being on my own. In the convent we were never allowed to be on our own. Even in the bathroom, someone was always walking in."

He sits down on the bed and says, "My friend and I had a drink. She showed me the de Sade letters, and then we got talking." The bride sits down beside him and puts an arm around his neck. She asks, "What were you talking about?"

"We came to an agreement," he says and begins to stride, long-legged, up and down the room. "We are going to edit them ourselves."

"Is that all you talked about?" she says, taking off her wet clothes and leaving them in a heap on the floor.

He looks at her and says, "We talked about my marriage."

She says, "Your friend thinks I am too young."

He says, "No, no, but you were not what she expected, you understand. She has known me a long time."

The bride wraps a towel around herself. She asks, "What sort of a person did she expect?"

She lies down on the bed and unwinds the thick towel, uncovering the soft curves of her young body. He stares down at her swollen breasts and wide, dark nipples. He looks into her eyes and raises his eyebrows inquiringly.

"I thought you knew about the situation," she says. "Mother said she discussed it with your mother."

He says, "She did say something about a quid pro quo. It doesn't matter" and lies down on the bed beside her. He cups her swollen breasts in his hand. He slips his hands down to her waist, her stomach, stroking the slight swell affectionately.

"What do you mean 'quid pro quo'?" she says.

He says, "They told you about my own situation. They set this all up. And about my friend, for instance. What did you think we talked about? There was never anything between us. There couldn't have been."

She looks at him blankly and asks, "Do you want to shower with me?" He rises from the bed.

She watches him as he lays his clothes neatly on a chair, holding his trousers by the hems and shaking them so that the pleat is preserved. He follows her into the bathroom. She stands with her head back, so the hot water falls on her face. He lathers her breasts, round and round. Then he bends over and does her stomach and between her legs.

He steps out of the shower and helps her out. He dries her body and leads her to the bed. She lies down, and he stands over her. She looks at the light hair on his broad chest, at his long, slim legs.

Suddenly she has the impression that she no longer recognizes him. For a moment she cannot think of his surname, the new one she had taken only the day before. Her body freezes. He lies down beside her, rubs his body against her, and nuzzles her neck. She does not recognize his smell. He kisses her cheeks, her sex. He puts his hand between her legs. Then he is on top of her in the customary position. He is pressing down on her, his chest plunging against her face, so that she can hardly catch her breath. He is grinding his hips against her wildly, but his sex is too limp to penetrate her. His face is red and swollen from the effort, his lips are folded, and he seems to be holding his breath. He looks to her as though he is concentrating on a difficult problem that he will do anything to solve.

STRUCTURE

RIGHT AFTER I HAD MARRIED AND MOVED to Paris, I telephoned Martha and asked her to come and stay. I told her I thought she would love the place we had found, a big sunny apartment with blue walls on the rue de Noisiel, near the Portuguese embassy.

"What about Mark?" she asked. "How are you two getting along?"

"I'm sure you two will get along famously," I said.

She said she would not be able to stay long, because she was planning a trip to Spain. I said she should stay for as long as she liked. Then, right after I had hung up, Mark came striding in the door. I told him I had asked Martha to come and stay with us. He said he didn't know if that would be such a good idea. The place was very small, after all—one ground-floor room with a partition, a closet, some wicker furniture, and a sit-up bath, for three people, two Siamese cats, and an azalea; we were supposed to be on our honeymoon. He wanted to know who this Martha was.

I told him she was a couple of years older than I, the same age as he. At school she had befriended me in a moment when I was notably unpopular, and I had always been grateful. I had spent half my school vacations with her, riding wild horses.

"She won't stay long. She wants to go to Spain," I said.

The night she arrived, we heard her get out of the taxi, slam the door, and the taxi driver shout "*Salope!*" as she crossed the street. She had apparently refused to tip the man, who had been very rude.

That night she and Mark began playing two-handed bridge for money. They smoked and argued and laughed half the night. I sat up and watched them play for a while, then retreated to the sit-up bath and tried to read a book while listening to them laughing.

I think Mark won most of the time. I'm not sure if that was why he liked Martha so much or if it was something to do with the noses—they both had prominent noses. I wondered what it would be like to have a nose like that.

Martha made an effort to go out and leave us alone as much as possible in the beginning. I suppose she thought we wanted to be on our own, but the truth is that whenever she went out, we fought. Mark was doing a junior year at Science Politique, but he said it wasn't necessary to go to the lectures. They were always the same, year after year, and you could get a printed version of the course, a *polycopié*, which the professor read from anyway. You could read it all by yourself at home. He told me that the French were interested not in content but in form. One professor had made a big impression on him by saying, "It's *all* in the structure." If you could structure a discourse, it was of no importance what the subject was. He always gave a tie as an example of the subject. Sometimes he would try it—structuring a discourse on the subject of a tie—but mostly he lay on his bed with a *polycopié* propped on his knees. Usually he fell asleep.

On my bed, against the opposite wall, I was trying to read the complete works of Proust, because Mark and his mother were always talking about the characters as though they were intimate friends, and I wanted to join the conversation, but Proust, who had such difficulty sleeping, had a soporific effect on me.

Even at night we fought.

After a while Martha stopped going out and just stayed home with Mark and me. She busied herself tidying out the closet where we kept the food and the clothes. Someone had given us champagne as a wedding present, and we drank that instead of mineral water. She swept the floor, which the Siamese cats scattered with the shreds of wicker they clawed off the furniture.

We planned to leave together for Spain in the spring and swim in the sea and lie in the sun on the beach. Martha's grandmother had a big house in Spain, she told us, where we all planned to stay. We were great planners. Martha and Mark pored over maps for hours and studied train schedules. Martha burned her face getting a preparatory suntan under a sunlamp, while I lolled in the bath and imagined the baby in a romper and a sun hat, sitting at the edge of the sea.

When the weather became warmer, we went to the outdoor pool at the edge of the Seine. We lay side by side on the concrete, the water shimmering, the strong smell of chlorine in the air. My stomach swelled like a small hill between the plains of their backs. Mark lay with his head on what he called my pineapples. Or he and Martha lay side by side on a rubber float, throwing each other into the water from time to time. Afterward, Martha would stand with her back to us under the shower, removing her bikini slowly, throwing it down piece by piece, while Mark and I clapped. She twitched her firm, plump hips like a girl from the Folies Bergères, while we laughed. We all laughed a lot and played around like kids. Before the swell became visible, people often thought we were all related.

The days began with Mark going out in his slippers to buy the croissants and the *Herald Tribune*—that was the big outing. Another was taking me to the doctor, so that I could get a check-up once a month. We took walks together through the streets of Paris in the evenings, and we did dares. We dared Martha to go up to the cashier at the movie theater and present the money in her mouth as if she were a dog. Martha dared me to crawl under the table in a restaurant and pretend to be a cat. Once Martha dared Mark to throw one of my shoes onto the roof of the Portuguese embassy. Maybe it still lies there, rotting.

Sometimes Mark would come into the bathroom and pull me out of the sit-up bath, making me drop my book. He would carry me, dripping, and let me fall onto the middle of Martha's bed. He would dry me and take me onto his lap and kiss me, half-naked, in front of Martha. He would take me on his lap and feed me *petite Suisse* with lots of sugar, crunching the grains with a fork. We were always fondling each other in front of Martha; we were always declaring our undying love. Martha was always listening as we vowed we would never stop loving each other; Martha was always watching as we gazed into each other's eyes. We made Martha promise that if one of us were to die, she would kill the other.

One night I awoke at midnight with the sound of rain on the window sill and the flow of blood on the sheets. I rose from my bed and slipped through the partition that separated our beds from Martha's. I climbed into Martha's bed as we had done at boarding school. I put my arms around her and held her close and felt the softness of her plump body, the tenderness of her smooth skin. I stroked her fine hair. I remembered the moonlit night, the sound of the night watchman's heavy boots crunching the stones beneath the dormitory window, and the beam of the torch lighting the hydrangeas.

This time Martha told me to go back to my bed. I fell asleep thinking of Martha's sun-streaked brown hair. I awoke at noon and lay facing the blue wall, listening to the sounds of the rain running down the gutters and the Siamese cats clawing the furniture. Martha had started to pack her things. She said she could not wait any longer, she was going to Spain, she had had enough of the rain in Paris.

She wrote to us from Spain that she had finally lost her virginity to a Spanish bullfighter. She said she had not realized there would be so much blood. She sent us a photo of her lover in the suit of lights, and Mark pinned it on the blue wall. He referred to the lover as Fernando the Bull. We made love with some passion beneath his photo, and I dreamed of the light in Fernando's smooth, dark skin.

LIGHT

"YOU KNOW I DON'T LIKE THEM" HE SAID.

"I didn't know," she said.

"Well, I don't. I never have," he said.

"I thought you liked them because I do. I was passing the shop, and I saw them. I couldn't resist." She gazed down into the basket.

"Well, I don't like them," he said, "I keep telling you I don't. In fact, if you want to know the truth, it seems to me there's something unclean about them."

"Unclean?" she said, and stared at him as he strode across the room.

"I don't know why. Something to do with the fur maybe," he said.

"I thought it would make you feel more at home here," she said, and leaned back against the whitewashed wall, and looked around the hotel room, with its bare floor, its wicker furniture, its red-polished terrace, and, in the distance, the dark sand, wild ocean, and vast sky.

She walked over to the twin bed against the wall and gently

placed the straw basket in the middle of the striped counterpane. She said brightly, "I thought I'd call them Minou and Minette."

"Oh, for Christ's sake," he groaned.

She looked down at the two sleeping Siamese kittens. One of the kittens stretched a paw and opened its avid blue eyes and miaowed plaintively. She could see the little white teeth and the pink tongue. "Look at them. Aren't they beautiful?" she said.

He looked at her and shook his head. "I think you're strange and, frankly, rather insulting."

"I thought they'd make you feel less alone here," she murmured, and stroked their soft fur.

"Alone? On my honeymoon!" he muttered, and went on walking up and down across the stone floor.

She went over to him, reached for him, but he pulled away and went to the other bed, which was pressed against the wall. Because of his height and the long loose limbs, or perhaps it was because of the whiteness of his clothes and his skin, she thought he looked too big for the low-ceilinged room.

His blond head almost grazed the wide blades of the spinning fan.

He turned his back on her. He said, "They make me wheeze, for Christ's sake. I can't breath with them around. I can't believe you'd do something like this, out here, in a hotel room."

She looked down at her bare legs, her sandaled feet, and said, "I'll take them back. I'll return them immediately."

He turned toward her. "There's no point in doing that. You can't do that now. Besides, knowing these people, they wouldn't take them back. I'm surprised they let you into the hotel with them."

"I don't think anyone saw me," she said, and went over to him and tried again to hold him. "Don't be cross, please."

He started to say something.

"I'll take them back," she said. "I'll make them take them

back. It's so simple," she said.

"I don't want you to take them back. I'd feel worse if you took them back now. Stay here with them. I'm going for a walk," he said.

"You just went for a walk!" she said.

"There's nothing else to do in this bloody country," he said, and slammed the door behind him.

When she had fed the kittens, she lay on the bed beside them and watched them for a while. They were sleeping, curled one into the other, and they seemed almost to glow as though lit from within. There was something about the way their slanting eyes were tightly shut that she liked. She stroked them gently and then rose, picked up the key, and left the room.

You had to pass through a long dark corridor to reach the heavy wooden door that opened onto the elevator. It was that dead hour of the afternoon when even the waves seemed lethargic, breaking with a muffled sigh on the sand. But the light was the same; it continued to burn with unrelenting ferocity.

As far back as she could remember, she had been surrounded by this light; it had warmed her, it had lit up leaves and branches and flowers, it had muffled sounds; it had cast deep shadows on the ground; she had carried it with her in her mind wherever she went. Now, through the haze of light, she stared at the thick green grass, the hibiscus bushes, the palm trees, the row of thatched rondavels, and beyond that, the endless stretch of sand which sloped down to a wild dark sea.

There was no sign of him.

She chose a table at the back in the shadow of the green awning and ordered a coffee from the waitress, a young black woman in a green uniform with a ridiculous white cap and apron who sauntered indolently through the tables, carrying a tray on her head. Her head was held high; one hand hovered near the tray. The waitress walked effortlessly, moved her hips with a soft easy roll, with a catlike grace.

Pamela took out her notebook. She wrote: *What men really want is someone to convince them they are never going to die.*

She sat and watched the waves dying on the sand in the fading light.

She turned on the light and stood at the door for a moment and surveyed the room. She gasped, and her shoulders slumped. She was still standing there, gazing, when he entered and stood beside her, and said, "Good God, did you do that?"

She walked on the dark sand toward a pool she had found in the rocks. Despite her sandals, she could feel the heat of the sand on her toes. The beach was pulsing with heat, and beads of sweat gathered in her eyebrows, but she was used to it; it did not bother her. It was never too hot for her. She walked on until she came to the pool. She clambered over the wet black rocks, removed her sandals, and sat for a moment with her feet in the water and stared at the beach and the sea. In the sun of the early afternoon, the restless sea shimmered darkly. The huge dark waves crashed against the rocks. They seemed to shake the earth and the air with their force. There was no shade, only the shadows from the rocks and, near the hotel, the changing huts on the edge of the beach.

There was no one in sight.

Everything was deserted in the high heat of day.

TRUST

ON THE WAY THERE HE THINKS OF WHAT she once said to him:
Never trust anyone completely, not even me. He has always
taken this as just another sign of her trustworthiness. Besides,
in the predicament he is in, he cannot think of anyone else to
trust.

For a moment, he hardly recognizes her. She is in a skirt
and a shirt with the top buttons undone, and she comes toward
him fast. She seems part of the crowd and yet separate. He has
always thought of her as too thin and a little dry. Now she looks
almost plump. When he kisses her cheek, she holds him tightly
a moment and then stands back. She shakes her head at him
the way people do; she clucks her tongue. She says, "You're
paler than a ghost."

He says, "You look wonderful."

She laughs and says, "Oh, darling, at this point, none of it's
real, it all comes out of a jar."

He says, "Thanks for coming all this way."

She says, "Darling, I'm delighted to be here with you," and
kisses him again; she looks him in the eyes and adds, "Besides,

I'm always glad to be of help."

It is barely dawn, the streets almost empty. The hotels are dark. All the great avenues run toward a star. Water rushes down the gutters. There is no sun, only a white sky. Early morning, the early morning in Paris.

She settles back in her seat, lights a cigarette. She still smokes through the thin tortoiseshell cigarette holder he gave her years ago. She says, "How warm it is here! I didn't think it would be warm so soon."

He keeps his eyes on the road.

He feels her hand on his on the wheel.

She says, "I know, sorrow seems incongruous in the spring."

"I am so lonely," he says suddenly.

She says nothing. He has a childish desire to burst into tears. He has seen his father weep in the same way, and, it occurs to him, for the same reason. It seems odd, considering the circumstances, that they would be the ones to want to weep.

She says, "What I wanted to ask you was what you were working on these days."

He says, "Couldn't get the backing I needed for the business, but I've been doing some writing."

She says, "Writing? Really? On what?" and turns her head away.

He tells her he is filling page after page with odd characters, insights, nonsense. The project is consuming his life.

When he stops the car and is about to open his door, she puts her hand on his sleeve. She asks, "What does she know?"

He stares through the window of the car. He hears a far-off dog bark. He thinks of his wife and the children waiting. He says, "Everything. She knows everything. I couldn't lie to her."

His mother raises her eyebrows. She taps him on the cheek. "You fool," she says. She tightens her grip on his arm and adds,

"That's going to make things much harder for me. It would have been kinder to lie."

The apartment is on the rue Guynemer, near the Luxembourg Gardens. It's a wide street. At this hour it is completely deserted, heavy with silence. There's a faint smell of wet tar. The chestnut trees are huge and black. In the leaves, blossoms balance like candelabra.

He is in love with this city. He likes the tree-cool avenues, the mist, the Indian-blue evenings. Sometimes he says, "The city is my soul." He believes, like the Gnostics, that when he dies what the angels will ask him is, "Where do you come from?"

They take the small elevator. Standing close, they rise slowly. The son looks at his mother. The nose is the first thing one notices in her face. It is his nose, a large nose that cannot be disguised.

His wife comes in from the veranda as he and his mother enter the room. The wife's hair is wet from the shower, and her eyes glisten. She greets his mother, who says, "Now, now, no tears." The wife calls the children, who are dressed as if for church, with ribbons in their hair.

The sun breaks through the cloud for a moment. There is the sound of the early morning traffic in the wet street. A dove rises with a beating of wings. The light shifts on the curve of the sofa and catches the round photo frame on the photo of the wife's father. With her arm around the father, she smiles up at him with the smile of the spoiled child. The apartment, with the mother in it, seems changed.

The wife closes the glass door to the veranda and brings in the birdcage with the canary. The wife says, "We bought two, a male and a female, and we called them Victoria and Albert, but Victoria died, or it might even have been Albert. It's hard to tell one from the other."

His mother laughs and says, "It must have been Albert!" The lone canary sits silently on the swing in the sun. "I don't know that it can live alone," the wife says.

As they go into the guest bedroom at the foot of the stairs, the son hits his forehead on a low beam and swears. His mother says to his wife, "I think it was terribly clever of you to find this lovely old place."

The son says he supposes his mother must be tired after the voyage, but she professes only hunger. She claims she has not eaten at all, that, really, the food on airplanes these days is hardly edible. As she talks, she takes out her hairpins, lets her long hair fall down her neck. She brushes her hair with energy. He suddenly remembers standing behind her in the hotel in Switzerland and brushing her hair as a boy.

His mother says, "I seem to be eating all the time, but I never put on any weight. Nothing seems to stick to these old bones." She asks is there something to eat in the house. Could the maid bring some food? What about a glass of sherry?

He raises his eyebrows and says, "There's no maid, Mother, only a cleaning woman, who comes twice a week."

His mother says, "No maid, good heavens, how do you all manage in this big old place?" The mother turns to the wife and says, "You ought to have someone full time. If I were in your shoes, I'd have two. I have to put up with my old daft Ines. Heaven knows what she's doing now, probably lying on my bed and eating sweets."

He watches the wife bring in a tray heaped with eggs, bacon, sausages, coffee, and beer, the china clattering against the glass. She walks slowly and smiles a wide meaningless smile. The girls follow her, carrying a loaf of black bread on a wooden board, giggling.

His mother claps her hands and takes the tray from his

wife. His mother says to his wife, "Darling, do come here and sit next to me. Here we all are, all of us together again, after all. Let's enjoy ourselves, as we always do. 'Life's a ware that will not keep,' someone once said." She puts her arm around the wife's neck. The wife kisses his mother and says, "I'm glad you've come."

The mother says, "Well, you don't look very glad, darling."

They sit around the table and sip coffee and watch the mother eat and drink. She gives a piece of toast to the youngest child, who eyes her grandmother warily.

"There's nothing like beer and sausage to restore the spirits," the mother says. She wipes the froth of the beer from her mouth. She draws her chair nearer to the wife's. "You must stop carrying on as if someone has died, darling. I know what you are going through, but it isn't the end of the world. You ought to get out of the house more. You look as pale as a turnip."

The youngest repeats, "A turnip! A turnip!" and claps her hands. The son laughs too, and even the wife joins in. She says she will have to go up to the shops to buy food for dinner.

"We'll all go with you," the mother says. "It'll do us good."

At the butcher's, the mother suggests they buy a loin of beef, a leg of lamb, and a plump chicken. She says, "We can have the lamb tonight. You must rub it with garlic, marinate it in wine and rosemary, coat it with flour, and cook it in a hot oven and serve it with those delicious little green beans—you know the kind I mean. I like it the French way, brown on the outside, and bloody inside."

The butcher is an elderly white-haired man. He wears a long bloodstained apron tied tightly around the waist. When you stand close to him, his eyes look watery. He chuckles and says he likes to see someone with a good appetite. He winks at the mother. She smiles, puts an arm around the son's shoulder and one around the wife's neck, and says, "I haven't seen them for almost two years, so we're entitled to celebrate, don't you think?"

The butcher nods and whistles and sharpens his knife; he sharpens his knife for so long it would cut up anything at all, the son thinks. He watches, as the butcher wields his long sharp knife with great dexterity, but fussily, with something of the old bachelor about him. He goes on whistling under his breath. He lifts his head to glance at the mother, leers a little, and says, "You have a very lovely daughter-in-law, ma'am, very lovely, indeed."

When the mother awakens from her rest that afternoon, she tells the son that she has had a wonderful idea; she has changed her mind about the lamb. The wife is to put everything into the freezer, and she, his mother, will take them all out. She wants to go to a place she remembers from a visit to the city years ago. She says, "It's out of this world, very romantic: candlelight, heaps of food, and there's dancing."

He says surely no one feels like dancing. The wife will want to stay with the girls. His mother tells him to call the baby-sitter and make a reservation at the club.

The narrow street near the place is crowded. All the traffic seems to have funneled into one street. The mother says, "Put a perfectly polite Frenchman behind a wheel, and he turns into a monster." She reaches across the son to blow the horn.

He says, "That's not allowed here, Mother." He feels hot and tired before the evening has begun. At the club, the mother enters first. She draws herself up importantly and motions to the head waiter, "That table over there," indicating a large table in a prominent place. "I'm afraid that table's reserved, Madame," the man says stiffly. The mother slips him a bill, and he ushers them to the table requested. It is lit with a ceiling light that casts a bright beam. The son blinks and looks around the room. The place is deep and gleaming. Polished wood lines the walls.

The mother orders champagne and caviar. She fills the wife's glass. The wife sits and stares vacantly ahead. She has vague blue eyes and white, even teeth. She obediently gulps down several glasses of champagne. She is in a dress she has not worn for a long time, it seems to the son, something black, and her skin glistens.

The wife says, "I'm feeling a little better now."

"Of course you are, darling. You probably haven't had a moment out in years," the mother says.

He watches as the wife rises unsteadily on high heels and disappears among the dancers on the dance floor. He turns toward the mother and says, "I'm worried about her."

The mother says, "Of course you are, but it doesn't make a bit of difference in the end, does it? It isn't what will help the situation, now is it?" She leans close to him. She cups one hand to the side of her mouth and whispers, "Darling, tell me, are you having fun? I do hope you are at least having a little fun. I mean we only live once, don't we? And, sweetheart, will you let me see her? I'm simply dying of curiosity. She sounds so very lovely. Very blond, you said, was that it?—and long, long legs. I can just imagine her. I'd love to catch a glimpse of her."

He says nothing.

She goes on, "Tell me sweetheart, I'm dying to hear, how ever did you two meet?"

When he has told her the whole story, the mother sighs. She says, "Look, I know how you feel. There's no stopping something of this sort. I've been there too, let me tell you. But you can stop pulling your hair out, you know; it seems to me your hair looks thinner than before, darling—you used to have such lovely curls. Soon you'll have no hair left, and then no one will want you."

He runs his hand through his thinning hair. He mutters, "I don't think anything could be worse than this. I spend my time rushing back and forth between them. When I'm with one of them, I feel I should be with the other. I keep composing letters of explanation in my head. I'm going to have to do something drastic."

The mother says, "Well, don't do anything drastic. Wait it out. I've just the thing for Sarah, you'll see. Where is she, anyway?"

The mother and the son look up to see the wife dancing. She is waving one hand at them and dancing with a man in a tuxedo. They dance a Russian dance, crossing their arms across their chests and kicking up their heels with the knees bent. Back to back, his wife and a strange man are dancing.

The mother says, "See what I mean?"

The son shakes his head and watches his wife dance with the man. Her large breasts rise and fall as she moves. She seems to bear no consciousness of herself, no coquetry. The son finds himself thinking of the time his wife lay naked beside him in a beam of early morning light, and he found the names of fruits for every part of her body.

Now she dances sensuously, white calves flashing. She has always danced well; she laughs at him for his awkwardness. She says, "Your head is too far from your heels, that's why you trip over your toes," and now she is dancing with another man. They look as though they have always danced together, the son thinks. He notices that the man has a full head of hair.

The mother says, "Well, she does have a lovely smile, I'll say that for her; she's got good teeth, too, and good legs, and when she gets herself all togged up like that, she looks all right. Don't forget, she's quite a catch."

The singer is singing an old song that seems like something long-awaited, something the son has been looking for.

He watches the man draw his wife against his chest and lean back. The dance floor is crowded, and from time to time the son loses sight of his wife. When the food arrives, she has still not come back. He says, "The terrible thing is she annoys me. The harder she tries, the more she annoys me. I find myself snapping at her."

The mother does not seem to have heard what he has said; she is finishing off the first course. She says, "You're a good boy. You've always been a good boy."

Scanning the dance floor for his wife, the son says, "Sometimes, when she smiles that big hopeful smile, I have a terrible urge to slap her face."

His mother isn't looking at him; she is looking at the couples dancing as she says, "I remember how you used to scare me sometimes. I would look into your eyes and think, he's capable of killing someone, I know he is."

He stares at the dancing couples, too, and says, "I remember after Father left how you used to wake me in the night. Over and over, you would wake me when you felt alone, when you wanted to talk to someone. I was only six years old."

She says bitterly, "I was so sick and so alone, and I didn't have money; no one was interested in me. I couldn't sleep. I would lie there for hours in the dark, weeping, in that horrible cheap hotel with the smell of cabbage and bad drains. There was no one to talk to." The mother goes on, "Sometimes I would get you out of bed when I couldn't bear it any longer; I'd hold you in my arms and think, I have him, at least I have him."

He bursts out, "Couldn't you have let me sleep?"

The mother says, "Isn't it terrible that the only thing children remember is the harm that you do them? They never remember the good things," and the mother starts eating again. She attacks the main course. She fills her glass. She drinks. She continues, "And you were difficult. You don't remember how difficult you were. We had to leave the hotel because you set fire to the curtains. You almost burned the place down. And do you remember you stole money from my purse?"

The son puts his hand on her arm as she reaches for more champagne. He says, "It's not good for you, you know, Mother," and looks around the room at the other diners.

He looks at his mother. He notices she has spilled butter from her cutlet down the front of her dress. He sees that people are watching them curiously. He looks around anxiously for his wife.

The mother wipes her mouth and says, "You've never really wanted to work hard, have you?"

He shouts, "Why do you say that? I've never wanted to do the sort of work you wanted me to do, and the things I wanted to do you didn't think were grand enough."

"But you like to live well, don't you? You've always had the *gout du luxe*," she says, and drinks again. She is working on the dessert now, a chocolate eclair, and looking at him from the side of her eyes. She is snickering nastily, "Perhaps she's gone off with that man. Then what would you do, my darling?"

He puts his head into his hands. He says sadly, "But she loves me; I really believe she loves me, and the terrible thing is, the worse I treat her, the more she loves me."

The mother says, "I wouldn't blame her if she did go off with another man."

He shouts, "You shouldn't drink! It makes you mean, it makes you mean as hell!"

The mother says, "You're not even any good, are you?"

He thinks suddenly but she is the one I want to kill.

He sees the wife coming back to the table with the man with the thick hair. Something in her face lights up the room.

The man slips an arm around her waist.

The wife says, "What's wrong? Did we interrupt something?"

The son says, "Where have you been? Mother's tired."

The mother has slumped in her chair, her eyes blank.

The man smirks—the son thinks there is something of the fox about the man's narrow face—and says, "We just went to get a little air," and swings a chair up to the table and sits down astraddle.

The son says, "We are leaving now. My mother's tired."

The room seems suddenly still. The music has stopped.

The mother looks up and grasps the wife's arm. The mother says, "What nonsense. He thinks I'm drunk, but I'm not really drunk at all. I'm having some fun." The mother says to the son, "We're having lots of fun, aren't we, darling?"

The wife looks from the son to the mother and back again. The wife says, "You don't look as through you're having much fun," and sits down with the strange man at her side.

The mother says, "What's your friend's name?"

The wife laughs. She says, "Oh, this is Charlie. He used to live next door to me when I was a child. Can you imagine?" Her eyes glitter oddly.

The mother says, "What a coincidence! We'll have to drink to that, won't we? Have some champagne, Charlie."

The son leans across the table toward the wife and whispers, "Mother's drunk. We have to get her home before she makes a scene."

The mother announces in a loud voice, "I'm fine, absolutely fine. I want to hear all about Charlie. Now tell me about yourself, Charlie."

The son slams his fist down on the plate. He shouts, "This is enough!" He can see the crowd is enjoying the scene.

The mother asks the wife if she would like something to eat. The wife says that, actually, she is feeling rather hungry after all that dancing. The mother says, "Of course you are, darling; order yourself a cutlet and order another one for me. I'm beginning to feel peckish again. We have all the time in the world."

The son watches as the wife eats hungrily. He gestures to the headwaiter to bring the bill. The son passes it to his mother. She puts on her glasses, looks at the bill, and exclaims, "I can't possibly pay this thing! This is absolutely absurd! There must be some mistake!"

The headwaiter says grimly, "I don't believe there has been a mistake."

The mother shouts, "This is highway robbery!"

The son looks at the bill, and says, "Mother, calm down. This is correct. After all, we've had a lot of food and champagne." He hands the bill back to her again.

The mother says to the son, "I'm sorry, but I'm not paying an amount like this. Besides, I don't have an amount like this with me. You'll have to pay," she says, and pushes the bill toward him.

He looks at the bill again. He looks at the wife, but she is leaning toward his mother, patting her hand soothingly.

"Thieves, the whole lot of them!" the mother exclaims.

"Absolutely," the wife agrees.

The wife drives the car home with the mother beside her, all the windows open. The wife drives fast through empty streets. The brakes screech. The son sits in the back and grips the seat. The night has grown cool and dark.

In the small elevator, the son closes the doors on them. It is like shutting a coffin. They stand huddled close. The son stares at the floor like a gambler who has lost all he owns.

In the bedroom, he lies naked on the bed—his arms, his legs, his throat.

He is becoming smaller and smaller.

The room is very dark.

He can no longer see the window, the trees, the gardens, or even the great avenues of Paris.

AFRICANS

MOTHER PREFERRED ZULU SERVANTS. She said they had been disciplined warriors. They were obedient, conscientious, and fiercely loyal. Their society was built on loyalty. They had had great, autocratic rulers, who were astute military strategists, and who conquered much territory in a series of bloody wars. There was Dingane. There was Dingiswayo. There was the cruel Shaka who armed his men with short stabbing spears and made them walk barefoot for greater speed and mobility. He taught them new military tactics and obliged them to remain celibate until they were forty. He ordered his impis to walk off a cliff to prove their loyalty. They were our Prussians, Mother said.

Mother preferred the men over the women because, she said, they worked even harder, did not fall pregnant, did not indulge in unnecessary chatter, and did not hesitate to perform whatever was asked of them. They rose before dawn to brush the carpets, to polish the silver and the floors, piling all the furniture in the middle of the room. They scrubbed the kitchen floor on their knees.

When they served at table, they dressed in starched white

jackets and trousers, which rustled as they floated quietly and efficiently about in soft sandshoes. Red sashes ran slant-wise across their chests from shoulder to waist and ended in tassels that dangled on their hips like decorations of valor. They wore white gloves and tapped an opener against the bottle to ask us what we would like to drink.

The Zulu my sister and I loved best was John Mazaboko. He called my sister Sk-Sk-Skatie because of the initials on her silver christening bowl, which he polished almost into oblivion. Whenever he saw her, he would chuckle as though they shared some secret understanding. We followed him around the house and watched him as he polished the floors and the furniture and the shoes, even the soles of the shoes.

He was unusually tall, and so strong he was able to catch the ancient armoire when it fell forward and almost crushed my sister as a small child. But his hands were gentle. Mother said he could not bear to hear us cry when we were babies and would beg the severe Scottish nanny to allow him to hold us in his arms.

He taught us how to ride bicycles and ran down the bank beside my sister under the flamboyants, waving the dishcloth at her and shouting, "*Khale, khale, Skatie*," warning her to watch out, as she wobbled along.

He told us stories about the Tokolosh, the evil spirit who lived in the fish pond at the bottom of the garden. He told us all the jacarandas in the garden were good except for the last one on the left, which was bad. We never went near it.

He was the one my sister called when she accidentally stepped on her beloved budgerigar, a small brightly colored parrot, which lay flapping its broken wings, on the floor. He took its pulsing neck between his fingers and wrung it swiftly. "Better like this," he told her.

He brought us freshly squeezed orange juice in the early

mornings, entering the nursery with a tray and the newspaper for the nanny, drawing back the lined curtains to let light into the room and wishing us a good morning with a grave, "*Sawubona*."

Once, the Scottish nanny, a diminutive woman, known as a "white nanny" to distinguish her from the black ones, summoned him to clean the inside of a malodorous cupboard. Wrinkling up her nose, she said, "It smells Zulu." He bent down from his great height onto his hands and knees and scrubbed the closet clean.

After our father's death, our mother withdrew, closed many of the rooms in the house, draped the furniture with sheets, and gradually fired all the other servants. Even the Scottish nanny was fired for stealing Mother's knitting needles and hiding them under her mattress, so that Mother would not find them. The nanny slammed the door behind her and mumbled, "These children would be better off in an orphanage." Only John remained.

It was South Africa in the forties, and he was looking after two little girls and their mother. He seemed sad. "He's not too pleased," Mother told us. "He's actually a bit of a snob, you know."

Sometimes, when we came indoors, we would find Mother slumped on the sofa, food trickling down her chiffon dress, a cigarette burning her fingers, an empty glass on the floor. We would call John, and he carried her to bed.

I can see him, in a brief moment of reprieve, leaning against the white-washed wall of the empty servants' quarter, smoking his pipe in the sun. My sister sits beside him on the red earth.

I remember my sister running into him in the narrow corridor after emerging from her bath. A slip of a girl despite all the food she consumed, she was totally naked. John lifted his eyes to the ceiling and gasped in horror.

For some years we did not see John except during the holidays. Mother sent my sister and me to a boarding school, run along the lines of an English school from the last century: we wore green tunics measured four inches from the knee, kneeling; we read nineteenth century authors and studied history that stopped before the First World War, which was considered too recent to be taught objectively. We slept in long dormitories, the little ones crying out for their mothers. My sister dreamed that she had passed John on the stairs without knowing who he was.

We were kept busy. We spent most of our time after class doing sport to combat sexual urges, and to learn team spirit. My sister, who was tall and athletic, won prizes. But ambition was not considered seemly for Christian girls. We were taught meekness(for the meek would inherit the earth) as well as obedience, diligence, and like the Zulus, loyalty. As our head mistress pointed out, most of us were destined to be mothers and wives.

When my sister told me about her decision to marry, I was living overseas with my husband, and home just for a visit. It was raining hard that afternoon, and hailing, as it does so often out there, and we could hear the hailstones beating against the long windows. We were in the big kitchen with the pull-out bins, where the flour and the meal were kept, near the small, dark pantry where the big sacks of oranges were stored. There was the familiar smell of wet coal from John's fire in the courtyard. The room was dimly lit, and John, as usual, was polishing the silver with a toothbrush. His head was bent, and he whistled softly as he worked, the newspaper spread before him. He lifted his head and tilted it with interest listening to us.

"Who is he?" I asked.

"A doctor, a heart surgeon," my sister said.

"You said you wanted to be a doctor, Skatie," John reminded her and chuckled.

My sister hesitated. "He's an Afrikaner. You can imagine

how much mother likes that." She paced back and forth, restlessly. Lightning lit up the room. "She's dead set against the match, thinks the family is *common*, and keeps talking about his mother being *too broad in the beam*. Some old girlfriend of my fiancé's called mother and begged her not to let me marry him."

John waved the toothbrush at my sister as he had the dishcloth when she wobbled down the bank on her bicycle for the first time. "What did this woman say?" he asked.

"She just kept saying, *Please don't let her marry him*." My sister went on, "He's really very handsome and clever. Passed his matric at sixteen. Did all his studies on scholarship. Father does something on the railways. Doesn't have any money."

"What is he like?" I asked her.

"Frank, brutally frank. It's refreshing. Do you know what I mean?" I nodded my head, and John stared down at the toothbrush in his hand.

At the wedding my sister stood in her white dress, the handsome groom and all the bridesmaids and flower girls at her side, on the stone steps of the church. Naturally, John was not with them.

My sister said, "Thank goodness Mother has let me have John."

"What did he say?" I asked.

"I didn't even ask him. I can't imagine starting up housekeeping or life, for that matter, without him. I don't know how you do without help. Mother will move to the cottage, and he will stay with us in the big house."

The next time I visited my sister, John greeted us in the driveway of the house. "*Nkosazana*," he said, addressing my daughter with the Zulu title of honor and bowing his head, holding her hand.

My sister told me that something had happened. We were

enjoying the December weather. The garden was green and filled with flowers: blue and white agapanthi grew by the pool, and the jacarandas were in bloom again. We were wearing our swimsuits, sandals, sun hats, swinging back and forth on the swing seat and sipping lemonade, the ice melting in our glasses. The shifting light from the water shimmered in the feathery leaves of the acacia tree. My sister paused, forcing me to pay attention.

"Go on. So what was it?" I said.

She had given a party for her husband's family, inviting all the brothers and sisters, uncles and aunts, and their friends. She had done the flowers, great bowls of arum lilies and peonies, and ordered champagne. John had roasted chickens, baked gem squash and apple pies. He had laid them out on the trestle table on the veranda, next to the bottles of champagne, which were lined up like soldiers on a field of damask. He was wearing his starched white uniform and the red sash with the tassel.

In the middle of it all, my sister noticed that her husband was not in the crowded room, so she went looking for him.

Her husband had seemed short-tempered that evening as he often was, saying it was because of fatigue, from the long hours in the operating room, or because of my sister's careless housekeeping. He insisted that she be at home every day for lunch, and complained there was no discipline in the house. They had argued over the state of his white linen pants. John had not pressed them properly, her husband claimed.

Now she could not find him.

It was a particularly fine night, the air warm, the sky wild with stars. She burst into his study, where she discovered him on the floor, embracing another man.

"It was such a terrible shock. His whole family was there, all of our friends. What could I do?" my sister asked me.

"Screamed." I said. "Kicked them in the balls. Turned them

out of the house. Made a scandal!"

"But I couldn't, you see. He would have been ruined, struck off the doctor rolls."

My sister's husband made their boy exercise in the morning to keep slim. He had him do sit-ups and scrub his fair skin with a loofah in the bath. When the boy brought his friends home to play, his father followed them into the changing rooms by the swimming pool and stared at them and touched them. The boy grew silent and sullen.

My sister asked, "Will you go to the lawyer for me? I can't. He follows me. He will find me anywhere. I am afraid of what he will do."

"Sorrow seems incongruous here," my sister said to me, as John brought us a cup of tea in the garden. It was late afternoon, and I was visiting again. All those visits, year after year, have run into one another. Only certain moments remain clear in my mind. By then my sister was keeping the shutters down and sleeping for hours in the afternoons. We could hear the flapping of wings, the cry of the swallows. Someone was singing in the bamboo. It was spring and already hot out there. The three of us, she, John and I, strolled down into the cool of the garden together and sat in the shade of the flamboyants, where John had taught us to ride our bicycles.

He had grown thinner over the years, his face gaunt, as though he had turned inward, and was bent on polishing himself into oblivion. Life in that house had worn away at his spirit. His slanting eyes had lost that glimmer of humor when he looked at my sister.

Now he sat beside us in his impeccable khaki trousers and shirt. Big, bulbous clouds floated across the sky. He looked at my sister and said, "Skatie, you are not eating enough, I keep telling you. You don't listen to me anymore. You are losing too much weight."

"How can I eat?" she said. She told us she had awakened one night and found her husband digging up the rose garden outside Mother's cottage in order to plant cabbages. He had thrown a glass at her, cutting her lip, the blood streaming down her chin.

Shortly afterward, my sister left for Rome and Istanbul. She wrote to me that she had met someone there. "He was at the airport, and I watched him stride across the runway. He looks like a David, Donatello's and Michelangelo's."

When my sister arrived back home, her husband found a letter from the Turkish lover and cut his wrists and lay at the bottom of the stairs and called John and all the children to come and watch him die. John came and clucked his tongue and shook his head and did what he was asked to do. All the children stood in a hushed circle with John at the bottom of the stairs and watched the blood running down their father's hands. My sister found them all there, unmoving, the light behind them, "like a chorus of angels in some medieval painting," she wrote. They rushed her husband to a clinic where he recuperated and came home to fly into rages if anyone spoke of Turkish delight.

He beat the children with a belt, especially the boy, broke his bones. He beat the eldest girl unconscious. My sister did not submit to his beating her or her children without a fight. She was stronger than he when she was angry, grabbing his hair and biting, kicking his shins.

Once, she had him at her mercy. He shouted for the servant.

"John, help me," he screamed.

They were in her bedroom, the long windows open on the lawn.

"Yes, Baas," John called and came as usual, swiftly and silently, looming in the doorway, watching my sister hold her husband, his arms pinned.

"What are you standing there for, help me, for God's sake," his master cried.

For a moment, John did not move.

"Do what I tell you. Put her on the bed."

John grasped my sister and pulled her down. At first she struggled, called out to John, "What are you doing!" but when he did not reply, and she saw no glimmer of response in his eyes, she gave up.

I imagine her lying on the blue silk counterpane, her face swollen as if she has soaked up water. All the delicate colors have run. She can hear the cries of children, see the sprinkler turning, a rainbow in the spray. Her hair blows across her pale forehead, a flush spreads over her cheeks like a stain. There is a scar on her lower lip. Her small chin trembles. Her eyes are round and strained, shaded by thick lashes, awash with tears, and as soft a blue as the silk beneath her. She looks up and sees the faces bending over her, a blur of black and white.

The white baas takes off his belt and beats her across her legs, her breast, her face.

—For John Mazboko

WATER BABY

MOTHER WAS ENTERING THE SLEEP she would never have to relinquish, while I was falling asleep in the arms of a stranger. I would never again see her draw her velvet curtains on the blinding southern sunlight.

Here, it is not fall but spring, and I feel its warm undercurrent through a thin, white gauze of mist.

I have not often been in a situation of this kind. I do not go out with men, or women, for that matter, but return from work quickly, bolting my door behind me on the small, furnished flat the university has found me. It looks onto a wall, not the flat fields, the endless line of a distant horizon, the weight of a wild sky.

Since my arrival here, I have left my books in dusty piles on the window sill. I have spent my evenings trying to work, correct papers, or translate. I have been weighed down by layer upon layer of sweaters at the rickety kitchen table before its grimy window. When I opened it, my papers drifted like leaves around my feet.

A kind colleague insisted I meet a friend of her husband's. She said, "He is a good man. Do you know what I mean?"

It seemed necessary to say I did, but I had no idea. I was not used to men, good or otherwise. I had grown up in a house full of women, my father hardly a memory.

So we are in the street in the light of a lamp. He is slender and his face glimmers. His suit looks gray, his hair almost white under the pale light of the street lamps. He is walking fast, turning his head, waving his hands, talking to me. I do not know what to say to this man, to any man, to a stranger. I am having trouble with my words, my clothes, my hands, my feet. I can hardly walk. I feel like the little mermaid who had to walk on feet for the first time, each step the stab of a knife.

He takes me into a Japanese restaurant. There is a large gold dragon on the wall and small, black, lacquered tables set close. He sits opposite me, and we drink sweet cherry wine.

I have difficulty concentrating on what he is saying. He is quoting certain famous lines in French: Henry IV's "*Paris vaut une messe.*" I am not sure of the connection. I am sweating, and I fear rings will appear beneath the arms of my striped silk blouse.

I am wearing a beige skirt, low-heeled shoes, and the pearls Mother gave me when I turned twenty-one. I do not wear make-up. I wear my thick blond hair cut very short. I have worn it this way ever since I had ringworm as a child, and the hairdresser cut it all off. He lifted me up to the mirror to show me the remains of my hair sticking up around my head, hedgehog-like. I screamed and climbed under the bed covers and refused to come out, wailing that I was too ugly.

As my mother has often told me, she is very beautiful, and I see it in her eyes: long-lashed and sultry, the nose: straight and small.

111

Her lips fold together like the petals of a flower closing on the night, as she watches the light linger in the starwild sky.

It happens this way: the fan turns uselessly stirring up hot air. The foam from Mother's lager lingers on her upper lip as she lays down her glass and looks around the table with her big, blank eyes. She leans forward toward the delphiniums. "Pet, come with me," she says. She pushes back the heavy chair with the clawed feet. She rises silently, her face very white, her small head drooping slightly, like a snow-drop.

My aunt watches warily as Mother takes my hand and leads me from the dining room through the long corridor with the Cries of London on the walls. Mother walks slowly, unsteadily, stiffly. I can hear her stockings brush one against the other as we go down the corridor past the grandfather clock with its golden angels, their trumpets held aloft, wound twice a week by the clock-winder, past the armchair in rosewood, all curves, past the shell-shaped cups in the china cupboard.

We go up the carpeted stairs, cross the landing into the cool of her scented blue bedroom.

"Where is my little Pet?" she asks me, looking at me with heavy-lidded eyes, reaching out her arms, dreaming known dreams. She knows where I am. A big blond girl—big enough to swim alone in the pool without my water wings, to teach my dolls how to swim, tying string around their stomachs and dragging them across the surface of the water, I know what she wants of her Pet.

I have been told the man has many degrees, and I am afraid I, a linguist, may make a grammatical error. I am convinced he is counting my wrinkles, though I am only in my early thirties. My face is stiff from smiling.

His face is neither young nor old. He has darkly bright eyes and smooth, pale skin; his eyebrows are brown, his eyelashes long like a girl's, his cheeks narrow. He looks like a young actor, playing the part of an old man with a white wig.

We talk, as people probably do in such situations, of our work, our families. He tells me his family comes from Europe. His father left Russia during the revolution, drove a taxi in Paris, sang in a cabaret in Constantinople. His mother made lamp-shades in Harlem. They had a siamese cat called Koshka which they lost. For years his father would roam the streets calling for Koshka. He speaks about his patients, the long hours he works, how he has little time for reading.

I tell him of my students, my difficulties getting them to read anything at all. I speak of Mother's garden, the alley of jacaranda trees, how I believed as a child they were all good trees except for the one at the end on the left which was bad.

After dinner, the man clears his throat and asks me if I would like to see his apartment. I try to think of some reason to defer, but the best I can do is to ask how I will get home, as though, like Cinderella, my time will soon be up.

I asked to go to boarding school at a young age and after boarding school I left the country. I claimed political reasons, the desire for independence, the wish to speak foreign tongues—all false. I went north, further and further north, further and further from the sun. I studied in foreign tongues.

"Why," a puzzled professor once asked me, "do you wish to pursue your studies in a foreign tongue? It would be so much easier in your own."

His apartment is narrow, on a narrow, cobbled street, in a secluded part of the city. We enter through a basement which serves as his office, he says. There is a potted plant and a small powder room, where I wash my hands. We go upstairs to the living room where we sit on his straight-backed beige sofa. I tell him about

113

Mother's gradual retreat from life, the drugs' increasing hold over her. He holds my hand in his with what I take for sympathy. I let it lie in his warm, dry hands.

I sit on the tapestried stool before the dressing table and watch as Mother draws the velvet curtains. She slips her pale chiffon dress over her head. She struggles with her boned corsets, breathing heavily. She draws them down and then up and then down again. Panting in the heat, exhausted, she lets her flesh fall free. She lifts her glass and motions for me to squirt a little soda water from the net-covered siphon. She swallows her pills, gobbling them down voraciously from the palm of her small hand, the white traces staining the edges of her lips like chalk.

I take off my socks, my smocked dress, my red bows.

He begins tearing at my clothes—or that is how I remember it. Undoubtedly he would tell this story differently. He drags my skirt around my knees. I feel as though I were sinking, down and down, drowning, caught up in seaweed, my hair rising around my head. I say angrily, "Is this where you fuck all your women?" He laughs and goes on fluttering my clitoris expertly.

I say, "If we're going to do this we might as well do it comfortably, at least." I am exhausted and want to go to bed.

He leads the way up further stairs. Naked, he pads beside me, carrying his clothes over one arm, his tie in his hand. I glance at his body. I do not know if he is handsome. He is not tall, but has broad freckled shoulders and pale slim hips, a smooth hairless chest. He reminds me of the Water Baby, from a book I read as a child. As I remember it, a sooty chimney sweep enters the clean, neat bedroom of a little girl and is released, transformed into a baby, free to play about in water all the days of his life.

The man says for some reason, "This is very informal." Up

and up we go, through a sleeping loft, and up more stairs into the bedroom.

The half moon window is frosted over but luminous in the light of the street lamp. I can hear footsteps and voices calling in the street. The ceiling is so low it is almost on his back as he rises over me. I look up at two stiff white statues of the German poets, Goethe and Schiller, who look down impassively.

When he comes he makes a small moaning sound.

It turns cold during the night, and in the morning soft flakes have fallen leaving a lip of snow on the sill.

My aunt says, "I have been trying to get hold of you all night. Where were you?"

"Is something wrong?" I ask.

"It all depends on how you look at it. Your mother died last night."

"How did she die?" I dare to ask.

"The way she lived," my aunt says, not unkindly. She tells me Mother was found with her arm flung across her face, the velvet curtains drawn on the garden, traces of pills lingering at the edges of her lips.

My aunt adds, "You mother has left you all her things, you know."

"The furniture? The house?" I ask as my room spins about me, the miscellany of things abandoned by visiting professors in their haste to depart: the wicker chairs, the backless sofa, the geranium shrunken in its rock-dry soil.

"The house will have to be sold. There are debts to be paid," she says. "As for the furniture, you will want to sell it, too, I presume," she adds.

"No," I say firmly, "Sell the china cabinet to pay for the transportation and send the rest to me."

"Where will you put it, dear?" my aunt asks. "I thought you

said you were in some sort of furnished flat."

The early morning light glitters on the snow as I run along the edge of the river. I run on, shouting, "No, no, no!" into the cold silent air. I am not referring to Mother's death but to the assault on my body.

I dream that I am back out there. Dogs bark mournfully behind closed gates. No one walks in the tree-lined street. Pale mauve jacaranda blossoms fall slowly and unseen to the grassy pavements. There is the light of early morning sun on the compost heap.

I do not recognize the old house at first. It is the white gate and the seringa tree that give it away. The Dutch door is there, dark green, with its bronze knocker. I stand before it and raise my eyes and see the old house in the full glare of gold light. I seem to see into the dark of the room: the mauve silk counterpane, the velvet curtains, the paintings with the goblins and fairy faces, the dressing table with the triple mirror.

I catch sight of a small beringed hand emerging from behind a drawn curtain. The hand flutters there in the bright light. Mother waves from the window, waving me inside with a sad helpless wave. Faintly I hear her cry, "Come back in. It has all been a mistake."

He telephones and asks if we could meet. I say I am very busy; I have papers to correct. He asks if we could meet in a few weeks time. I tell him to try me then, and I climb back into the bath. I spend a long time lying in baths.

We eat dinner out, a second time. He eats fast, we make love fast, and he falls asleep with abandon. In his Marlon Brando undershirt, his leg on my thigh, his damp hair curling at the neck, his face shiny in the lamp light, he looks as though he were a ghost.

We rise early, and he drives me to the sea. It is a still spring day and the white sand is smooth and bare. Wild lilies grow along the edge of the beach like candles. The water is silver and calm. Only ripples, hardly of water, more of light, break drowsily with a sigh on the sand.

We run and throw ourselves into the water. We swim a few strokes, and he reaches out and holds onto me. We float together on the surface of the water, our legs linked.

He has been working continuously at the hospital through several shifts, he says, and falls asleep heavily on the hot sand, his smooth white skin exposed to the harsh glare of the spring sun. I rub oil on the freckles of his shoulders. I cover his head with my hat.

When he wakes, he sits up and asks me if I might consider moving in with him.

"There would have to be love for that," I say.

Climbing under mother's covers is like diving into the warm, scented sea. I lie and try to make out the pictures my uncle has painted of goblins and fairy faces in foam, watching the dark ship of the dressing table with its triple mirror sail looming. Mother draws aside her nightgown of some diaphanous stuff and offers up her breast to me. I lie beside her delicate body and suck on her dry breast. Mother strokes my hair. She makes little moaning sounds. "My baby," she says, "You are my little Pet."

Nights I wait with a hand on the telephone, looking at the brick wall and the lights behind lowered shades, imagining people moving about behind them: mothers scooping up their toddlers with both hands, or walking them across the carpet, men in undershirts doing push-ups, the sweat dripping from their faces to the floor, couples slow-dancing to familiar melodies, their bodies pressed together.

When I learn that Mother's furniture is arriving, I call him to say I will accept his offer to move in with him.

A huge moving truck shudders down our narrow street. A drunken man staggers out of the door of the cab. The driver explains it is the only person he can find to help. Breathless, sweating in the summer heat, they move Mother's large English furniture, piece by piece, into my lover's narrow rooms.

Such density of furniture is unimaginable. There are the grandfather clock with the golden angels, carrying trumpets aloft, the fat chests of drawers, Mother's mahogany dining room table, the eight heavy dining room chairs with the clawed feet; there are the paintings with the goblins and fairies, the tapestried stool, the Matisse armchair, all curves, the shell-shaped cups.

When my lover arrives home he stands very still in the doorway, regarding the furniture which the movers have placed as best they could through the rooms of his apartment. "What's all this?" he says.

"Mother's furniture," I say.

He takes off his jacket, folds it carefully, and without a word to me carries two chairs, one under each arm, out into the corridor. I ask him what he is doing, but he does not answer. He continues putting the furniture out into the corridor piece by piece. I hang onto the last one, flinging myself across the top of the chest of drawers, grappling with him. I shout like a fish-wife, as they say. I scream. I pull my hair, but, sweating and straining, he drags the chest out with the rest of the furniture.

When the last piece is in the corridor and only the built-in bookcases, the statues of Schiller and Goethe, and the sofa where it all began remain, he sits down.

I put on my hat and climb over the chest of drawers in the

corridor to get outside. I wander around the streets for the rest of the night. The wet streets glisten. Water rushes down the gutters. In the hot, humid air, I stumble across the cobbled streets, scuffing my shoes. I am sweating, overcome with an immense fatigue. I can hardly walk another step. In the first faint light I look about, dazed.

As I lie beside mother at dawn sucking on her breast, my aunt enters the room. She walks across to the window. She remains still and upright, looking out at the garden through the chink in the curtains. Then she pulls open the curtains with a short, sharp gesture, filling the room with brilliant light and her clear disapproval.

"But this is my baby," Mother proffers in explanation.

My aunt turns her head slightly to glare over her shoulder, purses her lips and says, "Some baby."

I have circled back to my lover's apartment. It is in the district where the city's meat is sold. In the early morning light, I see butchers in blood-stained aprons carrying carcasses over their shoulders.

As I stand in his street, he puts his head out the window and waves to me. He is wearing his Marlon Brando undershirt. "Come back, come back in," he says. I look up at him, and in the bright light his face seems luminous.

We lie on the bare carpet, and I look up once again at the white statues of Schiller and Goethe. The room is empty, the walls white, even with the blinds closed. Everything is still. He lies still beneath me. I can hear only our slow, soft breathing. My body presses with abandon against his. I feel the sap rising in me; I am recovering my roots in his body. After years of fleeing, I have come to a halt. Then I am floating free, cast out into the ocean, the warm water bathing my body, wave after wave, filling my open, moaning mouth. I forget the dressing table, the triple mirror, the blinding light, Mother's soft, sweet body. I forget the dead weight of the past, the long anguish of living and dying.

ON THE MONEY

THE WIFE SAYS, "I DON'T WANT TO DISCUSS IT."

The husband says, "But you said you would. You promised. You have to."

The wife says, "I told you I don't want to talk about it. It's my money, after all. I'll do what I think best."

The wife lifts her glass, lets the stewardess fill it with champagne, helps herself to another salmon canapé. He says to the wife, "Alcohol is not good for jet lag."

The wife says, "Oh, for God's sake, just relax and enjoy yourself for once, can't you?"

He shakes his head, says, "You have to honor a promise. We agreed on the sum, didn't we?"

The wife says, "I don't have to do exactly what we agreed to. I have thought it over since then. A person can change her mind. It's just too much. It's a ridiculous amount of money. Besides, I didn't realize those lawyers would take so much of it, and that dreadful real estate man, and the taxes. I have never given that much to anyone. Not even my children."

The husband says, "Well, give some money to your children.

I think that you should give more to your children. Why don't you?"

The wife says, "Oh, shut up, won't you," pushes her seat back, draws the grey duvet up and over her chest and pulls her mask down to cage her eyes.

She spots the caretakers walking through the crowd at the airport to greet them. They seem smaller than she remembers them. Gianna is wearing a loose cream sweater. Michelino looks diminutive, like his name, in well-pressed pleated brown pants and a pink cotton shirt. They have the elegance of people who live beside the elegant, dress as the elegant do, but who are not, ultimately, elegant. The wife thinks the caretakers look young, or anyway younger than she or her husband, but then, she reminds herself, the caretakers are younger. She remembers them bringing out their album and showing her their wedding photos during a dinner at their house. They shake hands with her respectfully. The caretakers inquire about the trip. The husband and wife say how they are pleased to have arrived. Michelino says, "I was afraid you would never come back."

"But we promised," the wife says, and Michelino lowers his respectful gaze and looks embarrassed.

They all walk outside into the warm soft air. The wife takes a big breath. There is that familiar smell of some sweet herb she has never been able to identify.

In the car the husband sits in front with Michelino, the wife in back with Gianna. The caretakers offer lunch, their car, their home. The wife says no, they prefer the hotel, which is in town, so that they will not need a car. They are here for such a short stay, she says, and they have business in the town. They must attend to it immediately, so that they cannot make lunch. They have to go to the bank, before it closes. Besides, they have eaten so much on the plane. They will see the caretakers that evening for dinner, when they have accomplished their business.

There is a respectful silence in the car. The wife looks out the window. On one side there is the jagged coast line, the dark rocks, the smooth sea, the glitter blurred by a faint haze, on the other, the fields of wild juniper, the yellow flowers glistening in the gold autumnal light. Every year she has come back here, first with one husband and her children, and now with this one. She has been surprised each time to find it more beautiful than she remembered it.

The wife asks the caretakers about the German couple who bought their villa. Gianna raises her hand and puts the tips of her fingers together like a money bag in the familiar gesture all Italians use even when talking on the telephone. She frowns and says, "I don't understand why they let us go. First Michelino and then me."

"Perhaps they did not want anyone full-time," the wife says.

Gianna says, "It's not as though they lacked for money."

"That's true," the wife says and thinks of how the Germans paid in cash.

Gianna says, "They just wanted their own people, I suppose."

The wife sighs and shakes her head. Gianna begins to tell the wife about the changes the Germans have made to the villa, but the wife lifts a hand and says, "Don't tell me. I don't want to hear," and shuts her eyes.

The bank director has very blue eyes, thick black lashes, and an intense stare. He smiles at the wife through the glass door. He has replaced the director she remembers. He opens the door for her, and asks if her husband would like to join them, glancing at him pacing up and down across the green marble floor in the dark hall. The wife says quickly, "No, no, it's not necessary."

The director says, "I see," and ushers the wife into a small, sound-proof room with orange walls. She sits down. He sits opposite her behind the big wooden desk. "What can I do for you?" he asks. She leans forward in her chair and says in a low voice, "I would like half the money in lire and the other half in travelers' checks."

He nods and spreads his fingers. "As you like, Signora." He makes a call and goes out of the room for a moment. He comes back with a pile of Italian notes and the checks in a silver plastic folder. He says, "I thought five hundreds would be easier for you to sign." She nods her head and signs the checks fast, making her signature as short as possible. He asks if she would like him to count the notes. She nods. He starts to count, counting fast in Italian. She loses count.

At her request he puts the bills in a brown paper envelope and seals it. She puts the envelope and the travelers' checks in a pocket of her handbag.

When she walks out of the windowless room, her husband emerges from the shadows. He walks with the quick impatient steps of the doctor who has little time. He, too, always surprises her when she sees him after even a short absence. She never remembers how youthful he looks, with the smooth cream skin, the light freckles she associates with his race, which has always seemed to her both familiar and exotic. Sometimes his skin looks so smooth she thinks it looks like a mask. He is not tall but slim with a thick head of dark hair, a nose she thinks of as aquiline and soft, dark, rather close-set eyes. He smiles a crooked smile and inquires, "Done?"

"Done," she says, and they walk out onto the piazza, arm in arm. He squeezes her arm and says, "Good for you."

The sun does not have the strength of summer sun; there is a soft haze in the air, but the leaves of the olive trees are filled with gold light. A slight breeze nags at the hem of her dress. She kisses her husband on his smooth cheek. She says, "Let's just have a look at the shops, for a minute, and then we'll take a picnic in the launch to the beach."

The husband says, "The shops can wait until later this afternoon. We ought to check into the hotel now and put all this money away. It's not safe to walk around with so much."

She asks the hotel manager if she might put something in the safe. He, too, says, "Of course, Signora," and ushers her into a small room with a big blue bowl filled with white lilies. She can smell their strong, slightly cloying odor.

Her husband waits in he lobby with the luggage while the hotel manager opens the safe for her and takes out the box. The wife puts the lire in the box and takes the key. She keeps the travelers' checks in her handbag.

The wife looks around their big white-washed room. She admires the painted iron bedstead, the armchair covered in bright yellow linen and the embroidered cotton framed on the walls. She walks out onto the veranda into the sunlight and gazes at the pool below, which is shadowed by palms, purple bougainvillaea, and pink and white oleander. She says, "It's lovely, so lovely here, isn't it?"

The husband says, "You don't miss the house at all, do you?"

The wife shakes her head. "No, I don't, actually. Funny isn't it? I have always preferred hotels, anyway. You don't have to make your bed," she says. She picks up her handbag with the travelers' checks, opens and closes the drawers of the dresser and the cupboard doors. There is nothing that locks. She hunts in her handbag for a pen. She says, "I ought to write a postcard. Why don't you wait for me downstairs?"

The husband says, "Write the postcard later. We'll miss the boat."

The wife puts the handbag on the yellow chair by the door and slips on her navy blue swimsuit, her new light blue toweling shorts, and her expensive, gaily-colored, high-heeled sandals. She looks at her slim brown legs in the mirror, ties back her blond hair, and rubs cream into the lines of her upper lip.

The husband watches her and says, "I am glad you are happy." He picks up the key to the room and the basket with the food for the picnic. The wife picks up her handbag. The husband says, "Leave your handbag here. You won't need it on the beach."

The wife smiles nervously and says, "Oh, I think I'll just take it along with me."

The husband says, "All right, then give it to me," and puts the handbag into the basket with the key to the safe and the bottled water and the prosciutto sandwiches for the picnic. The wife takes the basket from her husband and slings it over her shoulder.

They walk across the wide piazza and down the steps to the pier where the small motor launch is waiting in the calm, clear water. The boat-driver wears starched white shorts and a white shirt and clean white shoes. He smiles at them. He has a mustache and a healthy, reddish face. He takes the wife's hand to help her into the launch. She steps unsteadily into it in her high heels. She turns to take the basket from the husband who passes it precariously, she thinks, over the water to her. She sways and then sits down, clutching the basket to her chest. The husband and wife sit closely, side by side, as the launch moves out slowly through deep blue water. The spray rises in the air. The rocks glisten. The low scrub glints, gray-green, spotted with yellow juniper in the mellow autumn light. The wife says, "This is such fun." She rises and stands with the basket slung over her shoulder, next to the boat-driver. The husband takes the basket from her and holds it on his lap. The wife speaks to the boat-driver in Italian: "What beautiful weather. October is the best time of year here."

The boat-driver asks, "You are English, I suppose, and your husband is—an American?"

"Yes, an American," the wife replies.

He asks, "Is this your first time here?"

The wife says, "Oh, no. I have been coming here for years. I used to have a villa, here, but I sold it last year."

The boat-driver says, "You don't have any of the headaches in a hotel."

The wife says, "Absolutely. I was tied to the villa. There was always something I had to do to keep it up. I had to pay care-takers all year round."

The boat-driver opens the throttle and says, "This is more amusing." The spray rises in the air as the launch speeds through the water and bumps over the wide white wake of another boat. The water splashes the wife's face. She laughs and licks the salt from her lips. Her husband says, "Be careful, darling." The wife sits down beside him and puts her hand on the basket.

There is a young English couple with a baby in the launch, as well as an older woman from Texas who films the rocky coast line, talking into the microphone on her camera. The young Englishwoman wears a transparent black robe and blood-red lip-stick. She holds her boy on her lap and claps his hands together as they bump over the swell; he laughs. The Englishwoman says, "I hear there was a kidnapping here last year."

The wife says, "Yes, a little boy was kidnapped."

The husband says, "Terrible business. The kidnappers held him for months and months. They even cut off his ear and sent it to the parents to extort ransom, before finally releasing him."

The Englishwoman clutches the baby to her chest.

The Texan leans across to tell the wife that she has trav-eled widely through Europe and Asia and Africa. She has seen Victoria Falls. She has seen so many places she cannot keep them straight. When everyone gets out of the boat and walks onto the white sand of the small crescent beach, fringed with wild grasses, she says, "What water is this? Is this the Adriatic or the Atlantic or what?" The boat-driver says politely, "This is the Mediterranean, Signora."

Apart from the Texan, the young English couple with the baby, and a man who sleeps, or seems to sleep, on a deck chair in the sun, they are the only people on the beach. The boat-driver pulls out the deck chairs so that they face the sun and retreats to the shade of a small cane hut up the hill, where he prepares his lunch. The wife can smell the ragù. It makes her suddenly hungry. She suggests they eat their prosciutto sandwiches, but the husband says he is not hungry yet.

The sun is warm, but there is an occasional cloud that passes and casts a shadow over the beach. The wife stretches out in her deck chair and takes out a book from her basket. She sighs, "This is the life." She watches the husband walking fast along the edge of the languid sea. It is very quiet: only the slight lapping of waves—hardly waves, little ripples—can be heard and the faint stirring of the breeze in the long grasses.

The wife slips her finger into her handbag and feels for the thick wad of travelers' checks. For a moment she thinks they are not there. She has not even taken the time to mark down the serial numbers. Then she finds them. She feels the sun go behind a cloud and looks up at her husband, whose shadow has fallen onto her. He says, "Why don't we take a run before we eat—and think of dinner tonight!"

The wife says, "What about our things? We can't just leave them here." The husband smiles and shakes his head at her.

He says, "Of course we can. No one is going to touch our things."

"Well, you never know for sure," the wife says and looks

along the beach at the young couple playing with their baby and the sleeping man. The Texan has already moved on, taken the boat back to the hotel. The wife pulls on her running shoes, and when her husband is not looking, quickly slips the travelers' checks out of the handbag and puts them in the pocket of her toweling shorts. The pocket is not quite large enough for them. She covers them with her hand, smiles at the husband, and begins to walk up the hill. He runs ahead of her along the steep white dust path that leads up into the scrub-covered hills. She follows, running along the path in the sun. She sweats and finds it difficult to run with her hand on her pocket. She lets it go, now and then checking to see if the money is still there. She stops a moment and tries bending the checks to fit them better into the pocket but is afraid of damaging them. She thinks of pushing them down the front of her bathing suit but fears the ink may run.

At the top of the hill she looks down at another small white beach below. The water is completely transparent, a pale turquoise at the edge, and she can see the white sand and the even sweep of the beach like the smooth arc of a bow. Not a breath stirs, not a leaf moves. No one is in sight, she could be the first person taking possession of the place. She is very hot now and sweating heavily. She runs down the hill to the deserted beach. She takes off the shorts and leaves them on a rock, plunging into the cool water. It is very salty and buoyant. She swims out, turning onto her back from time to time to keep the shorts in view, then strikes out for the horizon. When she comes back to the beach, she finds her husband there, waiting for her in the shade of a pine tree. Beside him lie her shorts with the checks.

For a moment the wife thinks the sun has simply gone behind a cloud. Then she realizes it has sunk behind the hills. Under the arcades the husband and wife walk arm and arm in the gathering gloom. The day has ended early, still and calm. There is not a breath of wind. They hear the echo of their footsteps on the stone. In the dim light the wife notices certain cracks in the whitewashed walls, and the colors of the paint take on a fake glow. At this season the place looks what it is, a recent development, ephemeral, in a perdurable land. They pass the Texan who walks by with her camera around her neck. She waves gaily to them and says loudly, "I am seventy-two, but I am still having fun."

The shops are garishly lit under the arcades and filled with expensive goods. The wife says, "You should at least buy yourself some shoes."

"No, no, I have enough shoes," the husband replies.

The wife sees an expensive black sweater, tailored at the waist; a bright red scarf, strewn with flowers; a tie with a pattern of blue boats bobbing on the sea; soft leather shoes in black and blue. She wants everything she sees. She says to the husband, "Meet me back at the hotel in an hour. I am going to wander around a bit on my own." She buys everything she has seen, paying with some of the travelers' checks. When she arrives back in her room, she slips everything except the tie into her suitcase. When her husband emerges from the shower she gives it to him.

"I'll wear it for the dinner," he says, smiling.

Gianna says, "The glasses are from the villa, Signora. You see we only use them on special occasions." There are blue wine glasses from the villa, bottles of white wine, frosted with cold, the starched white tablecloth, and pink carnations and orange lilies as a center piece. The wife thinks the colors of the flowers clash but murmurs how festive the table looks. She sees four places set and asks about the caretakers' child. Gianna says they have sent her to her cousins for the night. "An aperitivo," Michelino says.

They sit on the veranda in wicker chairs and stare at the lurid glare of the orange moon on the dark water, and the distant lights of the town stirring the thick dark. The wife clutches her handbag with the bills on her lap. The husband smiles and makes desperate attempts to speak Italian. The wife sees he is trying to put the caretakers at ease. She recalls his telling her how uneasy he had been made to feel as a boy because of his race.

Michelino brings out a tray with tall drinks of something orange with cherries and mint.

The caretakers speak to one another in local dialect which neither the wife nor the husband understand.

They all drink. The wife's head spins. She asks where the caretakers' daughter is at school this year. Gianna tells them they have put the child in an expensive private school to study languages. "Languages are essential," Gianna says. The wife, who speaks several, wants to say that languages are no guarantee of success, but instead nods politely and tells the couple how expensive private school is in America. She mentions a sum. The caretakers gape.

The wife asks how well the child does at her new school. Gianna shakes her head and says that she is not stupid, but that she does not like to study. They do everything they can for her, but she is never happy. All she wants is to go out with boys. The wife wants to tell Gianna that she is wasting her money on a child who is obviously slow and in the wife's opinion spoiled, but she nods and smiles understandingly, and says all teenagers are the same. She excuses herself and retreats to the bathroom, clutching her handbag.

It seems to the wife that the small bathroom has been retiled, and a shower installed. She lowers the top of the toilet, sits down, and tears open the long fat brown paper envelope with the notes. She slips out a thousand note from the others and pushes it into the pocket of her handbag. No need to exaggerate, she thinks, and who is to know, after all? She decides to take out another and pushes that, too, into the side pocket of her handbag. She thinks of the lovely leather suitcase in the window of the expensive shop on the piazza and slips out another note.

She rises and goes back to the dinner table.

Gianna is now serving from a heaped dish of risotto. There are pieces of lobster, prawns, octopi, squid and many other types of fish in the rice. The wife says, "This looks delicious." Gianna tells the wife the risotto was cooked in champagne. Michelino fills the wife's glass with the dry cold local white wine. The wife says to the caretakers, as she does ever year, "You should open a restaurant."

The husband is still smiling and struggling to speak Italian, but it sounds increasingly like Spanish and the caretakers do not understand what he is trying to say. "What are you trying to say?" the wife asks the husband in English, but he continues in Italian. Eventually it becomes apparent that he is talking about the wife's children, a subject about which the caretakers always politely inquire.

"Excuse me," the wife say, and laughs, "it must be the wine." She rises again, walks around the table with the white cloth and the blue glasses, and slips into the small bathroom. She pulls out a few more notes. The brown paper packet is beginning to feel rather light.

Gianna staggers in with a heavy white platter of baked fish cooked in paper and stuffed with herbs and surrounded by lemons and parsley sprigs. She serves the husband and wife abundantly from the tender white flesh. "That's far too much," the wife says.

"No, no it is very light," Gianna insists. The local *porcetto* follows the fish. The baby pig has been roasted in rosemary to a crisp golden brown. "Oh, I can't possibly eat all of that," the wife protests, as Gianna serves her a large and tender portion. Sweating, going in and out of the kitchen to bring clean plates, more knives and forks, Gianna now offers a salad of tender green leaves and radicchio. The dessert is a type of local cheese served on paper-thin bread and smothered with honey. Michelino refills the glasses. He insists on serving a strong liqueur that makes the wife choke and brings tears to her eyes.

The husband is attempting to convey his interest for the people of the island, the wife can see. He brings up the subject of the little boy's kidnapping the previous summer. He asks how the boy is faring. Gianna says, "The father wrote a book about the kidnapping and made a lot of money."

Michelino says, "Jewish people, of course."

Gianna glances furtively at the husband and says, "I am not sure he was Jewish, Michelino. He might have been an Arab, is it not true?"

Michelino shakes his head, "No, no, he was definitely Jewish. They are all like that. Made a fortune out of his own child's kidnapping."

The wife, too, glances at the husband to see if he had understood, but he goes on smiling. He has not understood, she is reasonably certain. The wife rises and retreats to the bathroom and removes a few more notes from the envelope.

Now the husband and wife rise, light-headed, from the table. The wife holds herself erect with difficulty, choosing her words carefully. "We can never repay you for what you did for us over all these years, but we wish to give you a token of our esteem," and she slips the thin brown paper packet under a vase on the mantelpiece. The caretakers smile and blush and look down at the floor and attempt to mumble their thanks.

Outside the husband says, "You did the right thing darling. They are good people. They deserved every bit of it."

PART FOUR

DEATH

CORRESPONDENCE I

The killed object, from which I am separated through sacrifice, while it links me to God also sets itself up, in the very act of being destroyed, as desirable, fascinating, and sacred.

—Julia Kristeva, *Powers of Horror*

DEAR K,

She told me once, "You are so full of surprises." She certainly would have been surprised by my writing to ask this of you. What I am asking will not be difficult for you. Is it not something you have already done? What you did to her was a rehearsal, as it were, and she the understudy for me. You see, I know more than you think about what you did to her. At all events, she was not the one worthy of your efforts.

I presume it was not difficult for you the first time, either (if that was the first time). It probably came upon you of a sudden, as they say. Perhaps there was a moment of exhilaration, a moment when you felt more alive than ever before. Probably you thought of it as the supreme embrace. Certain scenes from literature come to mind. But you would not know anything about those, I imagine, would you?

You must have guessed that I would have wanted this some-day. It must be something you have wanted to do for a long time. I have always felt you understood my desires. Did you not once say how alike we were? We even look alike. Like brother and sister, in fact, whereas she and I looked like strangers. At best she looked like a pale copy of the original; the negative. I have a portrait of us as little girls—one of those sentimental renderings, made of children of that class in those days. It hangs above my desk in a heart-shaped beaten-silver frame. She has her arm about my waist, I, mine about her neck. She smiles up at me with her forget-me-not eyes. Her pallid complexion. Her white-tipped eyelashes. The child-white hair.

I woke last night in this large empty room. Yes, yes, it occurred to me, you must have taken her by surprise. Did she cry out? What did she say? Was it in light or in shadow?

Did you know these are the questions she used to ask me about the act of making love? She was always asking me about that. I knew more than she did about it, naturally. She wanted to know how long it took, if I suffered, if I talked or cried out, whether I left a light burning.

You know she talked to me. Sometimes we sat up, huddled together in that hot room under the eaves, all through the night. Inevitably, she would speak of you. Some of it I would rather not have known, initially. Then I became interested. I asked questions. I gave her advice. But she only took half-measures. You do not take half-measures. You take all.

When Mother called me in the night with the news, I was not surprised. I had no desire to go out there. I said something about the endless voyage; the plane ride, the dreadful ferry crossing from the mainland, the boat black with soot, the seas rough at that time of year.

"Don't come then," she said, but, of course, I had to come. When I told my husband, he turned to me with his habitual courtesy of attitude, and said in his sweet voice, "How did he manage it?" You will understand how easily I can manage this. I have planned it in detail.

Let me tell you the few details you need to know. A person can come and go like a ghost here. The house is one of a row of identical town houses, situated on a blind street. It is very quiet except for the hour when the children escape from school. The town houses face the public gardens imperturbably in this most provincial of French settings. The window panes are small and face west. The dwelling itself is divided in half, with entrances front and back, linked by a long dark corridor. The floor slopes a little as you go along it. The big rooms have high ceilings and thick walls with heavy moldings—*patisseries*, my husband calls them. My room is at the back. This is where I work, and where I lie down at night, though I do not sleep much; I leave the lamp lit in order to read. The room is quite satisfactory—very different from those small, brilliantly lit rooms with their open windows and doors and thin walls, where we grew up.

Is it, shall I say, very discreet? The back entrance is the direct way to my room. You approach it through a small iron gate. Slip your hand through the bars and under the creeper and lift the lever gently from the inside. You will enter the back garden. My room looks over this garden, lit in the morning and early afternoon with wan sunlight. Today there is no sunlight because it is snowing, the first snowfall of the season. Light flakes fall straight from a white sky. The garden is swallowed up by snow. A lip of snow lies on the window sill.

My husband inherited all of this from his ancestors, who were Bretons from the *petite noblesse*. His ancestors are buried with the kings of France, you know, *chiens couchants* at their feet. My husband has, for my edification, explained many times and at length the differences among the nobilities.

You are not worrying about my husband, are you? You will understand that he does not often visit my part of the house. He receives his patients in the front rooms; I work in the back. We each spend our days listening. He listens to the murmur of hearts, lungs, joints. I hearken to morphemes and the like. What I spend most of my days doing is translating. I do French, Italian, Spanish. I have always thought Baudelaire's version of Poe far superior to the original. I do not feel obliged to keep strictly to the words before me, just as when you come to me to do what I am asking, I, her sister, will allow you certain imaginative departures from the procedure by which you gave her to her grave.

According to Mother, they found her unclothed body in the shade of the tamarind trees. A slight breeze was blowing, and it was pleasantly cool under the trees. It was the buzzing of the flies that alerted her to the presence of the body. A swarm of flies had already settled on the gaping wounds. How appropriate: her pale soft skin attracted insects all her life. Such vermin have always kept their distance from me.

Hah, but not to take me for some silkworm spinning a cocoon of lies to envelope you and bring about your metamorphosis. You are not the sort of person one lies to, are you? You are far too clever. I do not need to dispossess you to entice you into my territory.

I need you just the way you are, as the song goes, and just, I am sure you will agree, the way you need me.

Oh, do not construe this correspondence as the musing of an overheated imagination. Count on my good sense. Unlike her, my motto is *festina lente*. I like to run behind a faster runner and take shelter in his shadow until the end is in sight. Then I pass my quarry by. I like sunlight filtered through shutters, dappled light through leaves; I like concealment.

I accuse no one of anything, you realize.

The time to come to me would be at night. I retire early. We work until late afternoon, when we trot a bit around the public gardens. We circle them, our greyhound loping at our heels. Can you see the chestnut trees spreading thin branches against the white sky? In the distance the children sail toy boats. The band plays a waltz. We proceed one behind the other in our identical white hats, our gaze lowered to the stones at our feet. My husband prefers the landscape produced in Art. He never looks at things, and particularly, does not admire flowers. Even my photo, which he keeps on his desk in his consulting rooms, is one in which I am seen from behind.

We never quarrel; we are always extremely polite. In the evenings in the kitchen—a narrow shadowy room with a stone floor and stone countertops scrubbed with *Savon de Marseilles*, and rudimentary plumbing, we prepare a light supper, usually spaghetti in *bianco*, or a grilled fish fillet followed by poached fruit, in silence. The fellow is usually silent except with the dog. We vie with one another to cook the evening meal, moving around the narrow room like twin ghosts, skirting one another, mumbling to ourselves—he mumbles in French, I in English. Once, I let slip a good china pitcher that had belonged to his mother. He uttered not a word. This morning, too, as I heard him gashing with a knife to retrieve the last drop of jam from the jar, I put out my hand, and took the knife from him. There was never a sign of rebuke, reproach, displeasure.

We eat our supper on trays before the television while we watch the evening news. Sometimes he touches my hand, and he will sigh, a glimmer, I think, of hope in his pale blue eye. But each night I take the plunge alone, unarmed, naked, into that ocean where we meet the dead. It is not necessary to lock my door. Do you see how easily you could come to me?

Do you remember the first time you came? I was watching

from the window on the staircase. You walked up the driveway as though you were a tall man. Your clothes seemed strange; too tight in some places, too lose in others. You gave me the impression of coming from some other land, an alien. You had the arrogance she so admired. I watched you emerge from the sunset wood, and pass by the double row of tamarinds, where she was to die. I saw you gaze across the hills recumbent in the last of the light. The air was still. I watched you study the house. Did you suspect, even then, that I would one day ask you this?

The moths followed you into the hall. I could hardly see your face in the shadows. You might have noticed the disarray of flowers and baskets on the table there—Mother's half-finished pyramid of peonies and pinks in the soup tureen or the floor that was shiny and red from the wax and the ochre. You told the servant that you had come about the advertisement. I remember Mother putting down her porcelain cup and leaning toward you, an elbow on her knee, saying she wanted her daughters to have the advantages she had never had. You seemed surprised she had more than one daughter. Mother sighed and said what she always did about the difficulty of bringing up two girls on her own. I remember you saying that you could supply languages, much in the way of mathematics, and a certain intimacy with music.

I recall how you lifted your head and sniffed slightly and remarked on the luxurious presence in the house. Mother nattered on about the abundance of honeysuckle and jasmine that cover the glassed-in porch.

You walked indolently across the soft carpet to the Steinway by the French doors and opened the curtains a little to let in the light on the keys, adjusted the tapestried bench slightly, leaned back your head as though listening. I was struck by the fact that your hair seemed almost too black, matching your clothes. Even your tie was black. Surely black is rather hot for the tropics? What the regularity of your face made me think of was a mask.

We all waited while the moment gathered. Your timing as always was nothing less than perfect.

My husband's ancestors died for the French kings, you know, sunk in the mud in their heavy armor at Agincourt. They went on dying for the crown in the revolutionary wars. They were captured and drowned in pairs, tied back to back, or facing one another, the bottoms of the boats opening up beneath their feet.

Sometimes, when we were younger, she would try to imitate my walk, holding herself erect, lifting her soft chin.

But only our voices could be confused.

I see her face. I see the severed stumps.

Of course, I did make the voyage out. I took the plane and then the overnight ferry black with soot, barnacled, fat-bellied, clumsy. The passage was an unusually rough one for that time of year. The boat pitched and rolled in the humid, stifling air, and the soot fell in flakes. The only cabin available at such short notice was small and windowless, the bunks narrow as coffins. I was horribly sea-sick, rolling about all night, sweating, obliged to rush into the bathroom; I felt as though someone were taking my head and beating it against the floor.

We docked at dawn. I drove fast on the familiar road under the eucalyptus trees, still rocking from the boat, my head heavy, as though filled with some viscous liquid. The flat landscape was unexpectedly boring, burnt in patches by winter fires. The place looked different, as though I had never seen it before. There were no echoes. The tall buildings of the capitol, the treeless streets, the smoke-filled air might have belonged anywhere. Where was the lush beauty I remembered, where the scintillant scenery? When I emerged from the city, all I could see were dun fields, scorched earth. It was as if my own past had been stolen from me, shut away behind mirrors, and this was someone else's, hers, perhaps, and she someone I had only known distantly. I thought of how little I had known her, really, of how little I had cared.

The island seemed to me beautiful but barren, blanched by the sun. I prefer rain and wind, but I knew I should be thankful for such freedom from downpours and other meteorological caprices. The island offers other dangers. I remember how she was stung once by a wasp, driving in the car, and stung by a jelly fish as she was floating in the sea. Are there still so many jelly fish in the sea? The islanders have always seemed more African than European; they are suspicious after centuries of invasions, like most islanders, I suppose, and their proclivity toward kidnapping frightens me.

Mother was waiting for me in the hall of the big house. For a moment, as I stood on the threshold with the light behind me, Mother took me to be my sister.

Did you ask her to do it with you for the last time, as you did with me? I did not hear your knock at first. I was dreaming of nuns. In my dream I cut off my thick hair; I wore long dark habits; I tied wire beneath my breasts. Your knocking went on, discreet but peremptory, as I lay on the narrow bed in the blue room, my face in the pillow. I opened my eyes and turned my head as the door swung open. A thin line of saliva ran from my mouth, and my naked flesh was damp from the heat. I would not have cried out even if I had the time. I would not have moved. I had been expecting you. You fell upon me fast. I was not afraid. There was nothing strange or unpleasant about your frenzy. I feigned sleep, but I could see your whiteness glimmering, the blunt head of the slit-eyed thing staring at me. I felt you turn me. I felt your cool breath on my heat. Then your body covered mine like a shroud. I reached out to hold you with my hands, my arms, my legs, in the familiar sequence. It was her body, her physical presence I was holding onto tightly, not yours.

The first time must be the most difficult, surely. It is difficult to teach a soldier to kill for the first time, I have been told. I have heard stories of soldiers ordered to raise and train a pet and then to kill it with their bare hands in order to train them to kill for some higher cause. But afterwards some come to enjoy the act, I have read; some find in killing a sublime moment of escape, as in the sexual act, even a moment of ecstasy.

This room, you will find, is quite satisfactory for what we have in mind. I have an early Albers and an Oldenburg over the fireplace. Everything is in order: the books without dust, the champagne-colored carpet unstained, the windows clear. A certain fastidiousness, it seems to me, is warranted. After all, the last things seen should be pleasant.

Every morning I rise early. I eat a light breakfast, usually a piece of fruit: a green apple at this season or a pear, and a slice of dry toast. I drink a cup of lemon tea without sugar. I walk the greyhound. I make sure my pencils are sharpened and arranged in the silver beaker. I write in a different color for each language, so that it can easily be erased. I empty the wastepaper basket; I remove any speck of dust from the mahogany drop-leaf desk. I sit down at my desk and begin translating.

Did you notice her that first time she came down the stairs? She plumped down beside me, an arm around my waist. You were still playing the Steinway for Mother in your black clothes. My sister was in her socks. There was a hole in one of them and ink on her cheek. Did you notice her on the stairs with her arm around my waist, her head on my shoulder?

Of course, afterward, people tried to portray her as a kind of poor innocent. As far as I am concerned, she knew what she was doing. Even as she sat on the stairs that first day, she knew. She was watching you and dreaming, I could see, catching her long lashes between finger and thumb.

When you lifted your hands from the keys, Mother remained very still in that way that was habitual to her, her cheek resting in her hand, her little finger curved toward her lip. From where I stood on the stairs, I could see her face in the light. Her breasts glistened in her low-cut dress.

She did look young, as she tied on that wide-brimmed hat with a ribbon beneath her chin. The hat looked like a giant butterfly. She threw open the French doors and went down the brick steps. You followed. You stopped at the top of the steps. Was it Mother's voile dress fluttering against her body that stopped you?

We came behind you, giggling. Odd, is it not, to think of us giggling? We were always giggling, slapping one another's backs with giggles, punching one another's arms with giggles, pressing our knuckles to our mouths, laying our heads in one another's laps, giggling over a parrot in a bag or a nomad.

I remember how Mother presented us to you, turned to show you the rose garden, scintillant, in full bloom. She said, "These are my roses," and then caught sight of us giggling in the shadows of the tamarind trees. She called out to us, putting her arms about our bare shoulders, her nymphets, offering us up to you, saying, "And these are my daughters."

I can imagine how the three of us must have looked to you: that sun-shot moment, the mother standing between the two daughters, looking as though she were the eldest sister, the straw of her broad-brimmed Dumas hat flapping against her forehead, the meshed net with its small jewels confining the masses of thick black hair, the pearl-drop earrings, the shimmering bracelets, the flashing diamonds; the slender wrists turning, the tiny waving hands, the beautiful, glowing, made-up face. You must have known that the face, even when it would be scarred with age, would be more beautiful than the two on either side. You must have seen the thrust of the chin, the munificent mouth, the avid eyes. You would have seen me, taller than Mother, angular at sixteen, the dark scar from a birthmark burned from my shoulder, copper hair cropped like a boy's, skin tanned from being outdoors, eye-brows wide-arched and gray-green eyes inquiring. You must have seen me watching you warily, stirring, impatient to escape Mother's grasp. You would have noted in passing the younger girl, hardly a girl at fourteen or fifteen, plump and so pale-skinned she seemed transparent, the blue veins visible at the neck—a hot house plant, not fond of exercise even then, languid even then, liquid, leaning lazily toward Mother, the fine child-white curls clinging to the damp forehead, the pale eyes blinking admiringly at you.

Do not imagine that I did not see your gaze slide over her and rest on me. I shook your hand briefly and drew back as Mother gave her a little push toward you, so that she almost brushed against your chest. Mother had already decided on a home-grown, handsome music teacher who spoke foreign languages for her younger girl. She had come to that conclusion even as the younger sister shook your hand bashfully, white head drooping slightly in the shadows, snow-drop like.

Mother said the day my sister was killed was a beautiful spring day. The wild flowers were knee-deep, the trees new-green, the birds bright-winged. It was you who came to her room early that morning to make sure that she would be at luncheon the last day of my sister's life. Mother remembered waking early that bright day to the sight of you leaning against the jamb of the door. She had slept as she always did with the door open, and she said you looked like a shadow, dressed in black, with the light behind you, leaning against the jamb. She was glad to be wakened by you from a bad dream.

You came even before my sister came to say good-bye. Mother said she was going to say she would not be lunching, because she was so tired and because it was already so hot. She often liked to remain in her room with the shutters drawn in her silk dressing gown with cold cream on her face, without going through the whole exhausting business of bathing, applying cream, dressing, the long process of putting on her corset and her half petticoat, her hat and gloves. But when you asked her to join you at luncheon she said she would.

Mother had been dreaming of a crying child, she maintained. To dream of a crying child was bad luck, she knew, but she had thought the child in the dream was her elder child, the elder sister, I. She remembered the child as red-headed and green-eyed and willful. She was crying angrily, her big mouth red and ugly. Mother was trying to suckle the child, trying to quiet her.

You must have done it to her in the white glare of the sun, the vast sky; the sound of the waves, the screaming of the cicadas.

Ah, yes, perhaps I should mention that you need not worry about the body. My husband will probably take the death as self-inflicted. He has a very practical attitude toward death. He will find another wife, the sort of wife whom it is not necessary to support who comes with an income of her own. Whatever my husband decides to say about the body will be believed. People believe my husband, I assure you. I suppose there will be gossip; in a town of this size there is always gossip.

My husband is not particularly interested in money; his work, as he says, is honest work, and yet somehow, all of this honest work makes him very little money. Of course, my sister and I never spoke of money. Money was just one of the many things of which one did not speak. One did not speak of money nor, of course, of suffering. No one suffered. Everyone was always having a wonderful time. Sex, perhaps occasionally, might be mentioned, *sotto voce*, by the men or even a married woman, but money, never. Yet I know she was fascinated by gold shares; she would rush to get the newspaper, to follow the fluctuations of her gold shares. She possessed father's good business sense. She did far better than I did with her inheritance. Perhaps you are interested in her gold shares? I will give you your instructions.

On that morning, Mother was sitting up in bed in her pink silk nightgown, eating her anchovy toast and sipping her coffee. My sister came to say she was going into town for the day. She was wearing that short white sundress she wore in the heat. She was hatless, in sandals, and in a hurry. She looked so flushed, and her cheek felt so warm, Mother was afraid she might have a fever. Mother suggested she stay home, but she would not stay. Instead she did a sort of pirouette, rose up on the tips of her toes, held the sides of her skirt so that the hem of her dress lifted to show her pink knees and all the rest as she twirled. She gave a little wave and went out the door.

CORRESPONDENCE II

Travel light. I think it is essential these days to travel light, do you not agree? It avoids so much unnecessary delay at terminals. You will need, after all, no more than what you can wear: gloves, a dark raincoat; perhaps a hat with a brim to conceal your face.

You need not come equipped. I will provide the equipment. Naturally, there is the question of what we will use. I have thought of everything. I keep it in a French provincial armoire, what they call an *armoire bombée*. It will supply us both.

Did you simply go to the kitchen and take the knife? According to Cook, you were rummaging in a drawer with a preoccupied expression on your face in the middle of luncheon. She did not question you, of course. She thought you might have been hunting for a corkscrew or some remedy for indigestion. Mother had gone to her room to take her afternoon rest.

On the long flight up here you will hover in a no man's land, beyond sight and sound. Do not allow anyone to disturb you. Indulge in a preparatory rest. Lean back in your seat. Relax and enjoy the flight, as the steward always recommends. Ask him for a blanket, a pillow, a glass of Scotch. You might even indulge, under appropriate cover, in a little preparatory enjoy-ment. I recommend it as a way of avoiding over-excitement at the crucial moment. You will see what I have laid on in prepara-tion for your coming. There will be flowers, even a few white orchids for the occasion.

Mother rose that afternoon from her rest to the bitter smell of zinnias in the damp air. We learned as girls, you know, that one never decorates a table with zinnias because of their bitter smell. She went for a walk in the garden. It was there that she found the body, which she took for a moment in her shock and confusion to be mine. She saw the body under the trees amid those garish blooms. The stomach had been pierced so that the entrails had tumbled into the long grass. The ants had already begun to crawl in them.

My sister would have grasped greedily at her pierced stom-ach when she was stabbed. She would have held her blue entrails up to the afternoon light. She would have run her fingers through them as we used to run our fingers through Mother's jewels.

You realize that I get what I want. My sister was only the appetizer. Mornings, I would thrust my arm into the dark of the drawer in Mother's desk. I would take out her Craven A tin from the back of the drawer and run my fingers through the jewels. I would lift them up to the light. "You can have the yellow dia-mond, and I will have the blue," I would say to my sister, but in the end I got them all.

I would lie with Mother on her silk bedspread, sucking on her slack breasts, while my sister slumped on the dressing-table stool, trying not to watch, with that absent expression, eating slice after slice of anchovy toast cut into finger-thin strips.

Though my color was good, I was told I was anemic and needed to rest on my bed with a book in the afternoons. My sis-ter, despite her natural pallor, was told to pull herself together and get some exercise. On car trips I sat in the back beside

Mother, my head on her lap, smelling the faint bitter scent of her sex through her thin, flowered dress while she read me fairy tales. My sister, in the front with the driver, leaned out the window and counted the cornstalks.

It was I who was presented to the queen at the Court of Saint James with pomp and ceremony, my thick hair piled high on my head. The presentation photograph hangs on my bedroom wall. I wore a scarlet satin dress with a décolletage that caught the prince's eye. When I came up to curtsy, he stopped nodding off and leaned forward from his throne to ogle my breasts. They are worth the effort, don't you think?

The voyage will give you time to read this correspondence again. Be guided by it. The act is transcribed here like a symphony, every note in place. Enjoy the music. Think of me as the concertmaster who leads his orchestral colleagues from their midst. I will set the music in motion. You, as the conductor, will provide the structure to our pleasure.

Imagine our meeting. I see your plane circling in the mist. I see you stepping into a taxi at the terminal, leaning forward to direct the driver to the Gare du Nord. The taxi creeps forward at first and then races. The driver shifts gears abruptly, as they do in Paris, and stops short before the lights. You are jostled and bone-tired. I see you standing at the ticket counter, raising your eyebrows at the price of the ticket. You find a single seat by the window. You see the bare arms of trees spread supplicant against the sky. You change at Rennes and pace up and down on the platform. The sky is naked, the air raw. Your throat is dry from the long flight. Someone asks for a match. You watch it flicker and go out. It is growing dark.

Mother said she found the body amongst the zinnias in the late afternoon. She crouched down and cradled it in her arms, as if my sister were still a child. She pressed the face against her breasts, as if to comfort her. She felt the blood seep through the flowers on her dress. She felt like the murderer with all that blood on her. Then she was not sure what to do. She laid the body back on the ground. Only then did she realize that it was my sister and not I lying there, carved up like a white lamb.

When you arrive here it will be snowing. Watch the flakes, shapeless and slow, drift to the ground. A flake falls on your face like the light touch of a cold finger. You can hear the melancholy sound of the train. On foot you follow the river northward. The river is swollen with snow. You cross the bridge and see the lights fragmented on the dark, fast-moving water. You shiver a little. You would like a drink. You wonder if the people are watching you from behind drawn shutters.

You come to the iron railings of the public gardens. The gilt tips shine in the lamplight. You are startled by the dry sound of the beatings of wings as a nightjar rises into the air. The convent bells toll the hour. From the front it appears that all of the rooms are dark. The paint is peeling from the front door. The bronze knocker, once shaped like an animal's paw, is worn to a stump. You hesitate. You proceed around to the back garden, and you see the light in my room.

The day of my arrival you had drawn the curtains on the light. Mother told you she was not expecting my sister to come back for luncheon. Mother said that she was not worried, that my sister did not always come back at midday. You seemed distracted. Mother supposed it was the wind. The wind was blowing grains of sand up against the panes. You did not pour her sherry, although the cut-glass decanter was laid out on the silver tray. She poured her own.

My sister had said she was going into town for the day and would not be back. If she had kept to her plan, what would you have done? Were you so determined? Did it have to be that day?

We will not be subject to chance. We will plan in advance. We will structure the scene. I will see that nothing goes amiss.

We will take our time. We will neither rush nor will we draw things out unbearably. Timing, of course, is essential. I will tell you when to begin. I will keep my wits. I will remain calm.

My sister came in flushed and feverish. Her dress was unbuttoned, her straw hat in her hand. Dust covered her sandals. Her white curls clung to her damp forehead. You went into the dark dining room and sat down to eat. You rose from the table in the middle of the meal, napkin in hand, and went into the kitchen, Mother said.

Did I mention that I spoke to my sister on the telephone that day? She had called from town for my advice. I reassured her and told her to return at luncheon. She was grateful. Perhaps she anticipated the event that was to follow.

You will come through the back gate, remembering to slip your fingers through the creeper and lift the lever. You know I am waiting. The back door opens with the first light touch of your fingers. You hesitate, looking back at your footprints in the snow.

You peer into the dim light of a long vestibule. You smell the dampness and the wax. A door is ajar at the end of the vestibule. There is an impression of light, as there is when one approaches the sea from the woods. You hear pages turning. The damp, uneven floor slopes downward as you creep forward uncertainly, like a blind man drawn toward the light.

You enter this large, well-lit room. It is warm and quiet. Your eyes adjust to the light. You see bookshelves, a drop-leaf desk by the window, a fern in a brass-studded pot, a fire. Beside it I have laid a low table and set out silver candelabra, polished to a high shine. Candles will add a touch of drama to the scene. You see me standing by the window, staring out at the snow. At first you cannot see my face, as it is turned from you. You watch me draw the cream silk curtains slowly over one window and then the next. Then I turn toward you but do not acknowledge your presence. You look at the fine cheekbones, the high color, the slanting gray-green eyes. The pretty sister, you remember calling me once.

Do you remember the two sisters waltzing around the dining table? The silver bowl with ripe peaches and plums glinted in the sunlight. The room smelled of overripe fruit, honeysuckle, and jasmine. The warm trade wind blew through the open window. The white web of the curtains billowed, and the crocheted tablecloth fluttered around the rim. The sisters waltzed around the table to the "Graduation Ball," dipping and rising, throwing heads back and forth, linked and laughing, full skirts, lace petticoats, soft hair swirling in the white light like foam. They glided across the shiny, slippery floor. The younger girl's cheeks were flushed, her skin shone, and she called out to stop in her woozy, urgent, high-pitched voice, but the elder sister had her firmly by the waist; she held her sister's thighs against her own.

You can see my sister in the way I move and in the way my lips curve slightly downward. You notice how my loose copper hair reflects the light of the fire. I am wearing something red, diaphanous, with all my diamonds. You see my bare feet on the carpet as I turn and come toward you slowly. You watch my breasts rise and fall. You look up. Above me you notice the arched ceiling and the green light.

You think you have found the entrance to paradise.

Biographical Note

Sheila Kohler is the author of four novels, *The Perfect Place*, *The House on R Street*, *Cracks*, and the forthcoming *Children of Pithiviers*; as well as a collection of short stories, *Miracles in America*. Her work has been translated widely abroad and it has been published in England. She has won an O'Henry Prize, an Open Voice Award, and her story, "Africans," will be included in *Best American Short Stories of 1999*. Her short fiction has appeared in *The Antioch Review*, *The American Voice*, *Bomb*, *The Columbia Magazine*, *Fiction*, *The KGB Reader*, *The Massachusetts Review*, *New Letters*, *The Paris Review*, *Ploughshares*, *The Quarterly*, *Redbook*, *Story*, and *The Yale Review*. She was born in South Africa and now lives in New York City.

Books by Helicon Nine Editions

FICTION

One Girl, a novel in stories by Sheila Kohler
Winner of the 1998 Willa Cather Fiction Prize, selected by William Gass

Climbing the God Tree, a novel in stories by Jaimee Wriston Colbert
Winner of the 1997 Willa Cather Fiction Prize, selected by Dawn Raffel

Eternal City, stories by Molly Shapiro
Winner of the 1996 Willa Cather Fiction Prize, selected by Hilary Masters

Knucklebones, 27 short stories by Annabel Thomas
Winner of the 1994 Willa Cather Fiction Prize, selected by Daniel Stern

Galaxy Girls:Wonder Women, stories by Anne Whitney Pierce
Winner of the 1993 Willa Cather Fiction Prize, selected by Carolyn Doty

Return to Sender, a novel by Ann Slegman

The Value of Kindness, short stories by Ellyn Bache
Winner of the 1992 Willa Cather Fiction Prize, selected by James Byron Hall

Italian Smoking Piece with Simultaneous Translation by Christy Sheffield-Sanford
A multi-dimensional tour de force

Sweet Angel Band, a first book of stories by R.M. Kinder
Winner of the 1991 Willa Cather Fiction Prize, selected by Robley Wilson

POETRY

Flesh by Susan Gubernat
Winner of the 1998 Marianne Moore Poetry Prize, selected by Robert Phillips

Diasporadic by Patty Seyburn.
Winner of the 1997 Marianne Moore Poetry Prize, selected by Molly Peacock

On Days Like This, poems by Dan Quisenberry

Prayers to the Other Life by Christopher Seid
Winner of the 1996 Marianne Moore Poetry Prize, selected by David Ray

A Strange Heart by Jane O. Wayne
Winner of the 1995 Marianne Moore Poetry Prize, selected by James Tate

Without Warning by Elizabeth Goldring
Co-published with BkMk Press, University of Missouri-Kansas City

Night Drawings by Marjorie Stelmach
Winner of the 1994 Marianne Moore Poetry Prize
Introduction by David Ignatow, judge

Wool Highways, poems of New Zealand by David Ray
Winner of the 1993 William Carlos Williams Poetry Award

My Journey Toward You, poems by Judy Longley
Winner of the 1993 Marianne Moore Poetry Prize
Introduction by Richard Howard, judge

Women in Cars, poems by Martha McFerren
Winner of the 1992 Marianne Moore Poetry Prize
Introduction by Colette Inez, judge

Hoofbeats on the Door by Regina deCormier
Introduction by Richard Howard

Black Method by Biff Russ
Winner of the 1991 Marianne Moore Poetry Prize
Introduction by Mona Van Duyn, judge

ANTHOLOGIES

Spud Songs: An Anthology of Potato Poems to benefit Hunger Relief
Edited by Gloria Vando and Robert Stewart

Poets at Large: 25 Poets in 25 Homes
Edited by H.L. Hix

The Helicon Nine Reader: A Celebration of Women in the Arts
Edited by Gloria Vando Hickok

FEUILLETS

Limited editions of little books, ranging in length from 1–24 pages

Ancient Musics, a poetry sequence by Albert Goldbarth
A Walk through the Human Heart, a poem by Robley Wilson
Christmas 1956, a poem by Keith Denniston
Climatron, a poem by Robert Stewart
Cortége, a poem by Carl Phillips
Down & In, poems by Dan Quisenberry
Dresden, a poem by Patricia Cleary Miller
Generations, a poem by George Wedge
The Heart, a short story by Catherine Browder
R. I. P., a poem by E. S. Miller
Short Prose, an illustrated essay by M. Kasper
Slivers, a poem by Philip Miller
Stravinsky's Dream, a story by Conger Beasley, Jr.
This is how they were placed for us, a poem by Luci Tapahonso
Tokens, a poem by Judy Ray